Contents

PENGUIN MODERN CLASSICS

Chinatown

OH JUNG-HEE

Chinatown

Translated by Bruce and Ju-Chan Fulton

PENGUIN BOOKS

PENGUIN CLASSICS

UK | USA | Canada | Ireland | Australia
India | New Zealand | South Africa

Penguin Classics is part of the Penguin Random House group of companies
whose addresses can be found at global.penguinrandomhouse.com.

Penguin Random House UK
One Embassy Gardens, 8 Viaduct Gardens, London SW11 7BW

penguin.co.uk

Penguin
Random House
UK

First published in Great Britain by Penguin Classics 2025
001

Set in 11/13 pt Dante MT Std
Typeset by Jouve (UK), Milton Keynes
Printed and bound in Great Britain by Clays Ltd, Elcograf S.p.A.

The authorized representative in the EEA is Penguin Random House Ireland,
Morrison Chambers, 32 Nassau Street, Dublin D02 YH68

A CIP catalogue record for this book is available from the British Library

ISBN: 978-0-241-74436-9

Introduction

Oh Jung-hee (also known in English as O Chŏnghŭi) is the grande dame of modern Korean fiction, a writer whose works, spanning six decades, have drawn comparison with those of Alice Munro, Virginia Woolf and Joyce Carol Oates. In both technique and subject matter she remains one of the most accomplished of contemporary Korean writers. She uses flashbacks, stream-of-consciousness and a variety of narrative viewpoints to good effect. Her vocabulary is rich, her word choice deliberate and evocative. Her best stories are powerful, sensitive, carefully crafted portrayals of family relationships strained by unspoken emotions and unseen external forces. In these works, she probes beneath the surface of seemingly quotidian lives to expose nightmarish family configurations warped by divorce, desertion, insanity and death. Darkness is a physical presence in many of her stories, representing among other things these rents in the fabric of the family.

Oh is noted for coming-of-age stories such as 'Chinatown' ('Chunggugin kŏri', 1979) and 'The Garden of My Childhood' ('Yunyŏn ŭi ttŭl', 1980) and for intertextual stories such as 'Weaver Woman' ('Chingnyŏ', 1970), which echoes the folktale of the herder boy and the weaver girl, 'A Portrait of Magnolias' ('Mongnyŏnch'o', 1975), which includes a retelling of the Ch'ŏyong legend, and 'Fireworks' ('Pullori', 1987), which recounts the Koguryŏ foundation myth. In these ways Oh, like several other contemporary Korean fiction writers, connects strongly with Korean tradition while investing her stories with archetypes found in myth, legend and folktale.

Like Pak Wansŏ, Hwang Sunwŏn and Ch'oe Yun – three of modern Korea's most accomplished authors and each, like Oh, represented in *The Penguin Book of Korean Short Stories* – she emerged more or less fully formed as a writer. She began writing 'The Toy Shop Woman' ('Wan'gujŏm yŏin'), which was honoured with the 1968 New Writers Award by a Seoul daily, while still in high school. She then published approximately a story a year until her first collection, *River of Fire* (*Pul ŭi kang*), appeared in 1977. If by that time there were any doubts about her commitment to her craft, she dispelled them by remarking in a brief afterword to that volume that while writing a story she is constantly plagued by doubts as to whether she has given her all to that particular work. *River of Fire* is remarkable for the tension created by the juxtaposition in each of the twelve stories of a first-person narrative and a nameless narrator, an unsettling combination of intimacy and distance. In these stories, Oh became arguably the first Korean writer to carry out Virginia Woolf's dictum that killing off the gentle, egoless, self-sacrificing 'angel in the house' is part of a female writer's job.

The decade that followed was Oh's most productive period. Her second and third story collections, *The Garden of My Childhood* (*Yunyŏn ŭi ttŭl*) and *Spirit on the Wind* (*Param ŭi nŏk*), appeared in 1981 and 1986, respectively. The title story of *Spirit on the Wind* is a dual narrative that examines trauma from the point of view of the victim and her uncomprehending husband. The stories in both collections, like those in *River of Fire*, continue to portray families broken by desertion, infidelity, sterility, madness and death. These holes in the family fabric parallel the breakdown of a traditional agrarian society built around the extended family, a development accelerated by the industrialization of South Korea under a succession of military dictatorships from the 1960s to the 1980s.

By the mid-1980s Oh's writing had become more discursive as she responded to critiques of her works as lacking in historical consciousness and awareness of contemporary realities – two catchphrases applied indiscriminately by the conservative and patriarchal literary establishment of South Korea to writers who do not focus overtly on social, political, or historical problems in their fiction. Always an intertextual writer, Oh began to incorporate more historical elements into her works. 'The Monument Intersection' ('Pulmangbi', 1983), for example, is inspired by her own family's migration, after Korea's liberation from Japanese colonial rule in 1945, from Hwanghae Province in present-day North Korea to what would become South Korea.

A highlight of her literary fiction from the 1990s was the publication of her novella *The Bird* (*Sae*) in 1996. Earlier in that decade, in an effort to broaden her readership, Oh published two volumes of *conte*, a genre that in Korea consists primarily of family-centred miniatures and occupies an ambiguous space somewhere between literary fiction and popular fiction. She has also published children's and young adult fiction, and two volumes of essays.

The stories in this volume are centred in perhaps her most productive period – the late 1970s and early 1980s. 'Chinatown' is one of the most accomplished coming-of-age stories in contemporary Korea. 'Running Man', an early story built on her debut story, 'The Toy-shop Woman', focuses on the complications engendered by same-sex desire in a society still weighed down by strict neo-Confucian gender-role expectations. 'Mermaid' describes the psychological turmoil of a mother about to confide in her daughter that the girl was abandoned as a baby by her birth mother. 'The Garden Party' is a brilliant combination of manners, family dynamics and metafiction contextualized within a dinner party involving several prominent local families.

Oh Jung-hee will be remembered as the writer who pioneered gender parity in contemporary Korean fiction while raising the bar of accomplishment in fiction writing to a new level. She is one of the few writers of modern Korean fiction to acknowledge in her stories the individual's capacity for evil, and virtually no one has written more insightfully about trauma. It is difficult to overemphasize Oh's influence on contemporary Korean writers. Pyun Hye-Young (P'yŏn Hyeyŏng), one of the most prominent of the current generation, wrote her master's thesis on Oh. According to the dust jacket of Oh's 2006 essay collection, *The Patterns of My Heart* (*Nae maŭm ŭi munŭi*), among the authors most influenced by her is Kyung-sook Shin (Shin Kyŏngsuk), author of the best-selling *Please Look After Mom* (*Ŏmma rŭl put'akhae*, 2008). And the obligatory critical essay at the end of a 1994 volume of Oh's self-selected stories was written by none other than Kim Hyesoon (Kim Hyesun), contemporary Korea's most imaginative poet and a mentor to a generation of women fiction writers and poets. These accomplishments are all the more noteworthy when we consider that Oh's 'official' oeuvre of literary fiction (the works contained in the five volumes of her fiction published by Munhak kwa chisŏng sa in Seoul) consists of a mere three dozen pieces – thirty-four stories, a novella and a novel. That she has accomplished so much on the basis of such a comparatively slender output bears witness to her desire to make every work count.

Bruce and Ju-Chan Fulton
2025

Chinatown

Railroad tracks ran west through the heart of the city, dead-ending near a flour mill at the north end of the harbour. When a coal train jerked to a stop there, the locomotive recoiled as if in fear of dropping into the sea, sending coal dust trickling through chinks in the floors of the cars.

There was no lunch waiting for us at home on those winter days short as a deer's tail, so we threw aside our book bags as soon as school was over and flocked past the pier to the flour mill. The straw mats that covered the south yard of the mill were always strewn with wheat drying in the sun. If the custodian was away from his post at the front gate, we would walk in, help ourselves to a handful of wheat, leave a footprint on the corner of the mat and be on our way. The wheat grains clicked against our teeth and after the tough husks had steeped in our warm, sweet saliva, the kernels emerged, sticking like glue inside our mouths. By the time we reached the railroad they were good and chewy.

While we waited for the coal train we blew big bubbles with our wheat gum, set up rocks we had gathered from the roadbed and threw pebbles at them, or hunted for nails we had set on the rails the previous day to make magnets.

Eventually the train appeared, rattling to a stop with one last wheeze. We scurried between the wheels, raked up the coal dust, then hooked our arms through the gaps in the doors and scooped out some of the egg-shaped briquettes. Usually, by the time the carters from the coal yard across the tracks had made their dusty appearance, we had filled our school-slipper pouches with coal – the bigger and faster children used cement bags. Then, pouches and bags nestled beneath our arms, we hopped over the low wire fence on the harbour side of the tracks.

Our next stop was the snack bar on the pier, where we swarmed to the corner table. Depending on the day's plunder, our coal earned us noodle soup, wonton, steamed buns filled with red bean jam, edibles of that sort. Other times we swapped for baked sweet potatoes, picture cards, or sweets. Coal was as good as cash – something we could trade for anything around the pier – and so the children in our neighbourhood looked like black puppies all year round.

Our neighbourhood was Seashore Village to some, while others called it Chinatown. The coal dust carried in by the winter northerlies settled over the area like a shadow, blackening the sky and leaving the orb of the sun looking more like the moon.

Grandmother used to scoop ash from our stove, apply it to a fistful of straw, and polish the washbasin to a sparkling sheen before doing Father's dress shirts. But even though she hung the shirts to dry well inside the canopy, away from the dusty wind, she had to rinse them again and again and starch them a second time before she'd let him wear them.

'Damned coal dust! What a place to live!' Grandmother clucked.

A certain reminiscence invariably followed. I heard it so often I could recite it in her place: 'Let me tell you about the water from Kwangsŏk Spring. Now this was

2

in the North before the war, you understand. With that water the wash turned out so white it seemed almost blue! Even lye couldn't get it that white.'

When we returned to school after winter vacation our tutor group teacher took all of us Chinatown children to the kitchen next to the night-duty room. There she made us strip to the waist, assume a press-up position on the floor and endure a merciless dousing with lukewarm water. Then she checked for coal dust behind our ears, on the backs of our necks, between our toes and under our fingernails. An affectionate slap where the goose-flesh had erupted in the small of our backs meant we had passed inspection. We giggled as we slipped on our long underwear tops flecked with dead skin.

Spring arrived and with it the new school year. I was now in Year 3. My tutor group had classes only in the morning, and early one afternoon I was on my way home with Ch'iok, our arms around each other's shoulders.

'I'm going to be a hairdresser when I grow up,' Ch'iok said as we passed a beauty shop at a three-way junction.

Her voice reminded me of yellow. It was worm-medicine day at school and we'd been instructed to arrive on an empty stomach. I wasn't sure if it was my hunger, the medicine or the smell of boiling Corsican weed, but everything looked yellow – the sunlight, the faces of pas-sersby, the gusts that crept under my skirt and set it aflutter.

Except for several makeshift stores and the occasional skeleton of a bombed-out building sticking out like a decaying tooth, both sides of the street were barren.

'It was supposed to be the biggest theatre in town,' Ch'iok whispered as she pointed out the one remaining wall of a ruined building. Plastered in white, it resembled a movie screen or the curtain of a stage. But not for long. A work crew were taking aim at it with pickaxes and in no time the great white wall would come roaring to the ground.

Other workers were removing the reusable bricks and reinforcing rods from a wall already demolished.

'The area was bombed to kingdom come,' Ch'iok said, mimicking the adults and repeating 'to kingdom come' over and over.

Diligent as ants, the residents had reclaimed the devastated areas and were rebuilding their houses. Pots of Corsican weed boiled on heaps of coal briquettes in stoves made from oil drums.

Ch'iok and I constantly stopped to spit big gobs of saliva.

'Feels like the worms took the medicine and went nuts.'

'Uh-uh, I think they're peeing.'

Whatever it was they were doing, it didn't make us any the less nauseated. The froth from the Corsican weed, the smoke from the coal and the odour of plaster combined with the seaweed smell of the Corsican weed were one big yellow whirl.

'I wonder why they use Corsican weed when they're building a house,' Ch'iok said. 'One whiff and my head hurts like crazy.'

The arm looped around my shoulder dropped like a dead weight. I dawdled along, drinking in the smell of the Corsican weed. That yellow smell had been my introduction to this city, the very first understanding I shared with it.

My family had moved here the previous spring from the country village where we had taken refuge during the recent war.

'If your father could only get a job,' Mother used to mutter in between spraying her tidy stacks of tobacco leaves with mouthfuls of water. She would leave at dawn, a sack chock-full of those leaves strapped to her back, and return home looking half dead two or three days later.

'I don't give up easily, but I've had it with this damn tobacco monopoly. Unless you have a licence, you're always getting searched by the police. If your father could only get a job . . .'

Actually Father did have a job – looking up friends and classmates from the North who had migrated to the South and somehow managed to survive the war. Finally he got a real job, selling kerosene in the city.

The day the removal truck was to come, we ate breakfast at daybreak and then camped beside the road with our bundled quilts and our household goods lashed together with cords. Lunchtime came and the truck hadn't arrived. The endlessly repeated farewells with the neighbours were over.

Toward sunset, while we were plumped listlessly on the ground, fed up with playing hopscotch and land grabber, Mother took us to one of the local noodle shops and bought us each a bowl of noodle soup. The two oldest boys and I had changed into clean clothes before going outside that morning, but by now our runny noses had left a shiny track down our sleeves and on the backs of our hands.

It was dark now but Mother remained perched on the bundled quilts with our baby brother in her arms, glaring toward the approach to the bridge. Finally a pair of headlights appeared. 'It's here!' Mother shouted, and we children bounced up from where we'd been sitting on the bundles. The truck stopped, but only long enough for Mother to rush over to where the driver's assistant was sticking his head out of the passenger-side window. He shouted something to her over the roar of the engine and the truck pulled away. My brothers and sisters and I looked at one another in bewilderment. Those dark outlines towering above the high railing around the back of the truck were cattle. We could tell from the sharp, curved horns and the soft, liquid sound the animals made as they chewed their cud.

'They'll be back after they unload the cattle,' Mother explained to Grandmother. 'He arranged it that way because we pay half price if it's on its way back to the garage without a load.'

Grandmother nodded with a reluctant expression that seemed to say, 'I suppose you two know what you're doing.' We had never seen her disagree with Mother and Father.

A good two hours passed before the truck reappeared. After delivering the cattle to a slaughterhouse in a city ten miles away the men had had to clean the muck from the truck bed.

Mother and the baby squeezed in between the driver and his assistant after the rest of us and our baggage had been piled in the back. As the truck set into motion we heard the faraway whistle of the midnight southbound train.

I stuck my head out from the bundles and watched our village recede into the night and blend with the hill and its grove of scrub trees behind it. They undulated all together, a collective darkness blacker than the night sky but looking no larger than the palm of a hand, converging finally into a single dot that bounced up and down in counterpoint with the rear of the truck.

We crossed the township line and soon we were

barrelling along a bumpy hillside road. Those of us in the back, stuck among the bundles like nits, kept bouncing up like wind-up dolls. I figured the truck had lost its temper because of the driver's rough handling. Grandmother was doing her best to keep from crying out as she was jounced around. With each bounce I felt certain we were going to plunge into the river below, so I squeezed my eyes shut and drew my four-year-old brother close.

Though it was spring, the nighttime wind prickled our skin like the tip of a knife. Sweeping across the river, it raked my scaling skin with its sharp nails, at the same time ridding the truck bed of the odour of cow dung.

I thought of the soft, damp sound of the cattle ruminating in the darkness. 'Do you think all those cows are dead?' I asked my big sister. But she kept her face buried between her raised knees and didn't answer. Surely they'd been slaughtered, skinned, gutted and butchered by now.

The moon kept us company, and after a while my little brother shook his fist at it: 'Stupid moon, where are you goin'?'

The truck had to keep stopping to let one or another of us answer nature's call. To get the driver's attention we knocked on the tiny window between the cab and the truck bed. This brought the driver's assistant's head into view from the passenger window.

'What do you want?'

'We have to go to the bathroom.'

With a wave of his hand the man would tell us to go where we were, but then Grandmother would raise a fuss and the driver would reluctantly stop. The assistant would lift us down one by one and then bark at us to do our business all together. We shuddered in relief as we squatted at the side of the road. It took us a long time to empty our bladders.

Whenever the truck entered a different jurisdiction, which seemed to happen at every bend in the road, there was a checkpoint. A policeman in a military uniform would play his flashlight over the truck. Mother's tobacco peddling had left her with barely enough spunk to lean out the window and yell, 'Help yourself, but all you're going to find are a few lousy bundles and some kids.'

All night long the truck hurtled across hills and streams and through sleeping towns, and after stopping once for petrol, breaking down twice and going through a checkpoint at every turn in the road, we finally reached the city at daybreak. The streets seemed to perk up at the roar of the truck's antiquated engine.

At the far end of the city we arrived in a neighbourhood that seemed barely able to keep the sea at arm's length, and finally we were lifted down from the truck along with our bundles. After chasing us all night the moon had long since lost its shine and was hanging flat like a disc in the western sky. The truck had stopped in front of a well-worn, two-storey wooden house. The first floor looked like a shop with its sliding glass doors that opened onto the narrow street. 'Kerosene retailer' had been painted in red on the dusty glass.

This was where we would live.

I felt a blast of air so fresh and cold it made my teeth chatter. I was supposed to be looking out for my little brother, so I lifted him onto my back.

Rattling through the city on the truck, we had craned our necks from among the bundles and gazed out in curiosity and expectation. What we saw was different from what I had dreamed of in our country village. There I had equated the city with the rainbow-coloured soap bubbles we liked to blow from the end of a home-made straw, or else the Christmas trees we'd heard about in distant lands but had never seen.

Our street was flanked by identical two-storey timber-frame houses with tiny balconies. It was a shabby, filthy street but the squeaky wheels of the bicycles the sea-food vendors used to get to the wharf and the people tramping to work at the flour mill filled it with a chaotic energy, like when chickens flap their wings at dawn. The vendors and mill workers squeezed past the truck, which had planted itself in the middle of the street, and avoiding our carelessly discharged bundles they headed up the gentle slope that began at our house.

I was lost in confusion. Everything was so different from the country village we had just left. But had we really moved? Was this really our new home? It had a dreamlike smell that filled the sky like an evening haze. It was like a once-familiar dream now forgotten, only its impression remaining. What was that smell?

Father shoved open the door of the kerosene shop, then barked at the driver that he hadn't followed the terms of the agreement. The driver shook his fist at Father and pointed back and forth at the rest of us and our belongings. Curious and apprehensive, we could only gape at them.

There I was, a little nine-year-old with flaking skin. Beneath my gourd-bowl haircut and above the collar of my yellow synthetic jacket that was losing its batting you could see the bluish marks where the razor had scraped my neck. With my brother riding on my back, I looked around our new neighbourhood with a strangely uneasy feeling.

The neighbourhood had awakened at our noisy arrival. Heads with rumpled hair began poking out through windows and doors.

The dozen or so timber-frame dwellings that lined the street ended abruptly with our building. The houses facing each other on the hill above also had two storeys but were much larger. Some were white, others were blue-grey like faded ink.

The houses on the hill were spaced apart, except for the first one, which was enclosed by a broad wall that practically touched our house. Its door and all the windows I could see were too small and tightly shuttered. I wondered if it was actually a warehouse – no one could have lived there.

Those Western-style houses were strange, their steeply slanting roofs and pinched ridgelines looking out of place with their bulk. Perched on a hill that stood alone like a distant island amid the swarm of people on their way to the wharf, they radiated an air of cool contempt. Facing out to sea, their orifices closed tight like shells, they seemed somehow heroic even in their shabbiness. How old were they? What history did they contain?

The truck started up but didn't leave. The driver hadn't been paid to his satisfaction. He rested his arms on the steering wheel and shut his eyes as if preparing for a protracted battle.

'What's all this damn commotion so early in the morning? Are the Northerners invading again?'

The blunt, hard voice passed overhead, ringing in my

ears and silencing the menacing roar of the engine. Mother and then my brothers and sisters and I looked up to see a young woman on the balcony of the house across the street. Her legs were exposed to the thighs and an army jacket barely covered her shoulders. Her dyed hair swung back and forth as she went inside.

Father noticed my big brother scampering among the wheels of the truck. He grabbed him by the scruff, pulled him clear and rapped him on the head. Then he took in the sight of us standing in a bunch. 'Well, well, well,' he chuckled half in amazement, 'damned if we don't have ourselves a platoon here.'

Sunlight began to filter through the dawn clouds but still the shutters of the sleeping houses on the hill remained closed. As if collected from all over the city, a bluish gloom gathered ominously above the hill like clouds driven before a storm.

Finally the darkness was gone. The smell I'd first noticed, wafting through the delicate rattan blinds of the night, rose from everywhere in the streets like a deep breath at last exhaled. It was that smell that suddenly dispelled my confusion – the neighbourhood now felt familiar and friendly. At last I understood: embodied in that smell was a languid happiness, an image coloured by our refugee life in the village we had left the previous night, the memory of my childhood.

Later that year when the dandelions bloomed I was forever feeling dizzy and nauseated and had to sit on the shoe-ledge outside the door, spitting foamy saliva while my little brother crawled about in the yard putting dirt in his mouth. It seemed as if Grandmother cooked Corsican weed all spring long. When she forced a bowl of the broth upon me I drank it reluctantly, shaking my head in disgust before sinking into a languid stupor that felt like spring fever. The whole world was yellow, and regardless of the time, I was always asking Grandmother whether it was morning or evening.

'Are the worms stirring, you little stinker?' she would retort with a hearty laugh.

One day while I was descending into my yellow stupor, feeling like I was walking into a forgotten dream, the two-storey houses on the hill suddenly swooped close, one of the shutters opened, and the pale face of a young man appeared.

Mother was pregnant: this would be baby number seven. Fresh oysters and clams were the only foods that could soothe her queasy stomach, so every morning before school I set off over the hill for the pier, aluminium bowl in hand. I dashed by the firmly shut gates of the houses on the hill, sneaking glances at them out of curiosity and a vague anxiety, for those were the houses of the Chinese. A mere twenty steps down the other side of the hill the Chinese district abruptly ended at a butcher's shop and the pier unfolded before my eyes. I would stop to catch my breath and look back, and if I had timed it right the shutters of the shop would clatter open.

I went there every week to buy half a pound of pork. Mother would place money in my hand and send me on my way, always with the same warning: 'If he doesn't give you enough, ask him if it's because you're a child. And ask him to give you only lean meat, not fat.'

The butcher was a Chinese widower whose cheek sported a chestnut-sized growth. It looked as if someone had given him a terrific punch. Long hairs trailed from the growth, as if pulled by an unseen hand.

The first time I went there I found the man stropping his butcher knife.

'Are you only giving me this much because I'm a child?' I blurted. By standing on tiptoe I was just able to get my chin over the counter as I stuck out the money.

The man turned and looked at me, baffled.

Afraid he would cut the meat before I could finish saying what Mother had told me, I snapped, 'She told me to ask for lean.'

Stifling a laugh, the butcher quickly sliced the meat for me. 'Why only lean? I can give you some hair and skin too.'

Next to the butcher's shop was a store that sold such items as pepper, brown sugar and Chinese tea in bulk. It was the only general store in Chinatown. The people from our neighbourhood occasionally went to the butcher's shop for pork but didn't shop at the general store. We had no use for dyes and firecrackers and we didn't need decorative beads for our clothing and shoes.

The store's shutters were opened on one side only, and even on bright, sunny days the interior was dark and gloomy, as if enveloped in dust. But in the evening the Chinese flocked there, creeping like dusk through interlocking alleys. The women had great thick ears and wore silver earrings. They tottered on bound feet, baskets over their arms, their heads bobbing and the tight buns of hair resembling mounds of cow dung.

While the women shopped the men sat in chairs in front of the store and silently smoked their long bamboo pipes before creeping back home. Most of them were elderly.

We children parked ourselves in a row on the narrow,

low kerb, tapping our feet on the street and pointing at the men.

'Look at those dirty addicts – they're smoking opium.'

And in fact the smoke scattering from the pipes was unusually yellow.

Now and then the elderly men gave us a smile.

Our families lived right next to Chinatown but we children were the only ones who were interested in the Chinese. The grownups referred to them indifferently as 'Chinks'.

Although we had no direct contact with the Chinese in the two-storey houses on the hill, they were the yeast of our infinite imagination and curiosity. Smugglers, opium addicts, coolies who squirrelled away gold inside every panel of their ragged quilted clothing, mounted bandits who swept over the frozen earth to the beat of their horses' hoofs, barbarians who sliced up the raw liver of a slaughtered enemy and ate it according to rank, outcast butchers who made wonton out of human flesh, people whose turds had frozen upright on the northern Manchurian plain before they could pull up their trousers – this was how we thought of them. What was inside the tightly closed shutters of their houses? And what lay deep inside their minds, seldom expressed even after years of friendship? Was it gold? Opium? Suspicion?

'Let's do our homework here,' Ch'iok said when we arrived at her house. She looked up toward the quilt and blanket stretched over the side of the second-floor balcony. This was a sign that Maggie was out. If she were in, she would have been in bed, beneath the blanket. I hesitated, glancing across the street at our house. Mother and

Grandmother referred to Ch'iok's house as a whorehouse for the GIs. Our house was the only one in the neighbourhood that didn't rent out a room to a prostitute. These women threw open their doors to the street and thought nothing of letting the American soldiers give them a squeeze. Stained blankets and colourful underwear festooned with lace hung on the sunny balconies, drying from the free-spirited activities of the previous night.

'Scum!' Grandmother would say, turning away from the sight. To her way of thinking, women's clothes, and especially their underwear, should be hung to dry inside.

Ch'iok's parents lived downstairs and Maggie rented the big room upstairs with a darky GI. Ch'iok had to go through Maggie's room to get to her own, which was small and narrow like a closet. When I went to get Ch'iok for school in the morning I always encountered Maggie lying in bed with her hair dishevelled and the huge darky sitting hunched in front of the dresser trimming his moustache with a tiny pair of silvery scissors. Maggie would beckon me in with the slightest motion of her hand, but I always remained outside the half-open door, peeking inside while I waited for Ch'iok. The thick flesh of the soldier's chest looked like moulded rubber and his eyes were smoky. He always mumbled when he spoke, and he never smiled at me. What a gloomy man, I thought.

'Can't you call me from the street?' Ch'iok once asked. 'He doesn't like you going up there.'

But every morning I walked up the creaky stairs and called to Ch'iok while hovering outside Maggie's room.

'Maggie said she won't be back till tonight. We can play on her bed,' Ch'iok cajoled me.

I thought for a moment: Mother had a bad case of morning sickness and was probably lying in the family room, looking vexed about everything. My older brother had likely gone outside to catch mole crickets. And I knew that as soon as I walked in, Grandmother would tell me to piggyback my baby brother, who had just been weaned, and then shoo me out of the house.

So I followed Ch'iok upstairs. Jennie, Maggie's daughter, was asleep on the bed. Curtains kept the sun out and the room dim.

Ch'iok opened the storage cabinet, located a box of cookies, took two of them, and carefully replaced the box. The cookies were sweet and smelled faintly like toothpaste.

'That's so pretty,' I said, pointing to a bottle of perfume on the dresser.

Ch'iok turned it upside down and pretended to gently spray her armpits. 'Made in America.' Again she reached inside the cabinet and rustled around, this time producing two sweets.

'Tastes so good,' I said.

'Mmm, because it's made in America,' Ch'iok answered in the same blasé tone.

Jennie was now wide awake and watching us.

'Jennie, aren't you pretty? Now we have to do our homework, so why don't you go back to sleep for a little while?' Ch'iok spoke softly, brushing Jennie's eyelids down with her palm, and in an instant the little girl's eyes had closed tightly like those of a doll.

Everything in Maggie's room was marvellous. Ch'iok let me feel each of the belongings just for a moment, and every one of them brought a joyful exclamation from me as I caressed it. Then we replaced each item, leaving no sign that we'd tampered with it.

'I have an idea.'

Ch'iok reached inside a cabinet at the head of the bed and took out a gourd-shaped bottle half full of a green liquid. After making a line with her fingernail on the side of the bottle to mark the level of the liquid, she opened the bottle, poured a small amount into the cap and handed it to me.

'Try it. It's sweet – tastes like menthol.'

I quickly drank it and returned the cap to Ch'iok. She filled it for herself and gulped it. That brought the level of the liquid about two fingers below the mark. Ch'iok made up the difference with water, capped the bottle and returned it to the cabinet.

'Perfect! How was it – tasty, huh?'

The inside of my mouth was nice and warm, as if I had a mouthful of peppermint.

'Now don't tell anyone,' Ch'iok said, as she removed a velvet box from among some clothes in one of the dresser drawers.

Everything in Maggie's room was a secret.

The box contained a pearl necklace long enough to make three strands, a brooch adorned with garishly coloured glass beads, some earrings and other jewellery. Ch'iok tried on a necklace made of thick glass beads and studied herself in the mirror.

'I'm going to be a GI's whore when I grow up,' she said decisively. 'Maggie said she'll give me necklaces, shoes, things to wear – everything.'

I felt like the tips of my fingers and toes had gone to sleep and I was dissolving. I was short of breath and couldn't keep my eyes open. Was it the darkness of the room? I imagined the peppermint leaving a white trail every time I breathed out. I drew aside the curtain covering the door to the balcony and seething yellow sunlight came in, illuminating the dust and making the room look like a greenhouse. I touched my burning cheek to the doorknob and peered outside. Once again I saw the two-storey house in Chinatown with the open shutter and the face of the young man looking my way. A mysterious sadness, an ineffable pathos began undulating in my chest and then it spread through me.

'What's the matter? Are you dizzy?' asked Ch'iok, who knew what the green liquid was and how it affected you. She snuggled up beside me against the door to the balcony.

I shook my head, unable to understand, much less explain the feeling I had in response to the face in the second-floor window, and the next moment the wooden shutter thumped shut and the young man disappeared from view.

The glass beads of Ch'iok's necklace clicked together, their colours dancing in the sunlight. Ch'iok took one of the beads in her lips. 'I'm going to be a GI's whore.'

I drew the curtain and lay down on the bed. Who could he be? I tried fretfully to revive my memories of a forgotten dream. I knew I'd seen him the previous autumn at the barber's. I'd had to sit on a plank placed across the chair because I was so short. I had instructed the barber as Mother had told me:

'Please make it short and layered on the sides and back but leave it long on top. I'm ugly enough already, so a gourd-bowl haircut is no good.'

But when I looked in the mirror after the barber finished, I still had a gourd bowl.

'Too late to complain. But I'll do better next time – promise.'

'I knew this would happen! Why can't you concentrate on cutting hair instead of gabbing with everybody?'

The barber jerked the plank away from under me. 'What a smart-alecky little girl. That's no way to talk. I'll bet that yap of yours was the first thing that came out when you were born.'

'Don't you worry about how I should talk. And I'll bet you're a hair chopper because you came out with scissors around your wrist.'

The other customers roared with laughter. I looked around with a triumphant air. The only ones who weren't laughing were the barber and a young man sitting in the corner with a bib around his neck. The young man was studying me in the mirror. *He's Chinese*, I suddenly thought. Although I had seen him only at an angle from across the street, never close up, his inscrutable gaze had given me that impression. I took the towel from around my neck and tossed it in front of the mirror. Then I stamped to the doorway, put my hands on my hips and turned back: 'Until the day you die you'll be nothing but a hair chopper!' And then I ran home.

Father was constantly remodelling our house, as if to compensate for the privations of our refugee life in the country village – the entire family crowded into a single rented room, and before that the many sleepless nights he had spent keeping the children warm in his arms under a bridge or inside a tent. He got rid of our tiny yard, adding a room and a veranda to the house in the way that girls who have just learned how to sew might add secret pockets to the inside of a book bag or the underside of their clothing. And so a mazelike hallway appeared inside, long and narrow like an ant tunnel.

Along with the hallway there materialized a place where I could hide and no one would find me – the back room next to the toilet, where we kept old clothing, household stuff and various odds and ends. The day of the ill-fated haircut, I ran home, sneaked into that room and pressed my face against the narrow mouth of a jar, hoping in vain that the sorrow sweeping over my bones like a strong current would empty into it.

Several times after that, usually when I was hunkered down in front of Father's shop waiting for the evening newspaper, I sensed that the young Chinese man had opened his window and was looking toward me.

'Jennie. Time to get up, Jennie – your mom's here,' Ch'iok said in an affectedly sweet and gentle tone. Jennie opened her eyes and sat up. Ch'iok fetched a basin of water from downstairs. Jennie didn't cry even when the soapy water got in her eyes. We combed her hair, sprayed her with perfume and changed her into clothes from the closet. Jennie's father was white and her mother Korean and at the age of five she still hadn't begun to talk. She couldn't feed herself, much less put on her own clothes, and what she was fed tended to trickle out of the side of her mouth. When the dark-skinned man was there Jennie had to be moved to Ch'iok's room.

Grandmother occasionally noticed Jennie on the balcony or outside the house. 'Whelp!' she would say, looking at the girl almost in amazement, her eyes filled with the hatred she reserved for fur-bearing animals. She frightened me when she stared at Jennie like that. Some time ago, after our house was infested with rats, we had got a cat. The cat bore a litter of seven kittens in the back room. Grandmother fed it seaweed soup to help it recover, then stared right into the cat's eyes and repeated like a refrain, 'Kitty had some baby rats, seven baby rats.' That evening the cat ate all seven kittens, leaving only the heads. Then it yowled all night long, not bothering to clean its bloodstained mouth. As if she'd expected this, Grandmother wrapped the seven tiny heads in newspaper and sent them down the sewer drain.

Mother used to tell me that the reason Grandmother was so heartless and cold was that she'd never had children of her own. She was actually a kind of stepmother to Mother. I had once overheard Mother whispering about Grandmother to an elderly woman who was a distant relative: 'They were married only three months when that father of mine had an affair with her sister – can you believe it? That's why they separated and she eventually decided to come live with us.'

Jennie was like a doll to Ch'iok, who could give her a bath and change her clothes every half hour and never get a scolding from Maggie. To Ch'iok Jennie was sometimes a baby, sometimes a sick little girl, sometimes an angel. I envied Ch'iok with all my heart and it must have shown on my face.

'Don't you have a sister too?' Ch'iok asked me dubiously.

'She's my stepsister.'

'You mean that's not your real mother?'

'My stepmother,' I lied with a lump in my throat.

Tears gathered in her eyes. 'Well. Somehow I had a hunch. Don't tell anyone but I have a stepmother too.'

There wasn't a soul in our neighbourhood who didn't know this.

I linked my little finger with Ch'iok's and we promised to keep each other's secret.

'Does your mum beat you and tell you to get lost and drop dead?' I asked.

'Yeah, when no one's around.' Ch'iok lowered her trousers and showed me her bruised thighs. 'I'm going to run away and be a GI's whore.'

How often I wished I really were a stepdaughter so I could run away whenever I pleased.

Mother was still carrying baby number seven. None of us children in this poor district next to Chinatown believed that babies were brought to earth in the arms of an angel in the middle of the night. And they didn't emerge with bright smiles from their mother's belly button. Everyone knew a baby came out screaming from between the naked legs of a woman.

GIs in T-shirts were doing target practice with knives on one of the tennis courts at the army base. The knives cut through the air like silver needles toward the concentric circles on the target, giving off a piercing glint, a flash of light, a brightness like a man's prematurely white hair. Whenever a knife whistled to the black spot dead centre in the target the men howled like animals while we children gulped in terror.

There was a white GI who took a step back every time he hit the centre of the target. Once again he took aim, but as the knife was about to spring from his hand he suddenly pivoted and the weapon slashed through the air toward us. We flattened ourselves, shrieking, against the wire fence surrounding the base. I felt a warm wetness between my legs. A moment later we lifted our pallid faces and saw the chuckling GI pointing at something behind us. We turned and saw a black cat rigid on its back, legs in the air, the knife stuck in its chest. The cat was the size of a small dog, probably one of the strays that were always getting into the garbage cans on the base. Its pointed whiskers were still trembling as we crowded around it. My big brother picked up the carcass and ran off. The rest of us took off after him. My wet underpants chafed.

When we were out of sight of the Americans' barracks, my brother stopped, panting. He looked down at what he was holding, shuddered and let the cat drop. It fell to the ground with a thud.

'What did you bring *that* for?' one of the children demanded.

Thus challenged, my Little Napoleon of a brother pulled the knife from the cat's chest and wiped the blade on the grass. It was a folding knife, the blade sharp and pointed like an awl. He snapped the blade into place and put the knife in his pocket.

'Go get me a stick,' he commanded.

One of us snapped off a branch from a tree we had planted the previous spring on Arbor Day and brought it to him.

Brother took off his belt and looped it around the cat's neck, then tied the end to the branch. Down the street we paraded, the cat splayed out behind my brother, its paws dragging along the ground and its weight bending the branch on his shoulder like a bow.

By the time we reached Chinatown the long summer

day was waning. As the sun slanted toward the horizon the cat's shadow grew out endlessly from its midsection.

The flour mill workers walked past us on their way down the hill, their hair frosted with flour, their empty lunchboxes rattling.

We headed toward the pier, treading on each other's gigantic, frightening shadows and that of the cat's black, elongated carcass. And then I saw him again. The second-floor shutters were open and he was watching our procession. I couldn't fathom his gaze but I thought I saw sorrow, anger and perhaps a subtle smile.

When we reached the pier Brother set the branch down and took the belt from around the cat's neck. Spitting in disgust, he looped the belt around the waist of his trousers, which were constantly threatening to fall down. Then he dropped the cat into the mass of garbage, empty bottles and rotting, white-bellied fish washing up against the embankment.

As we often did around sunset, we decided to go to the park, where we liked to lie on our stomachs on the endless expanse of steps and look up the hoop skirts of the GIs' whores, exclaiming at the bare legs inside the bloated framework of whale tendon. Or we would loll on the grass and bellow one of the old standards an ageing prostitute might sing to herself:

> Looking back at my youth I see every step of
> the way stained with tears,
> Looking back at my regrettable past I hear the
> bells of Santa Maria.

But this time we walked up silently and deliberately toward the sky.

At the highest point in the park stood the bronze statue of the old general whose landing operation here just a few years ago was already inscribed in legend. From this spot the entire city could be seen. Boats and ships were moored at the pier, their flags fluttering like confetti, the jaws of a crane biting over and over into their cargo. Off in the distance floated a vessel that was probably a foreign freighter but looked more like an islet or a huge old carp.

The bell from the Catholic church behind us kept tolling. That tolling had been tugging at us ever since – no, even before – we'd thrown the cat into the sea. Producing endless waves of sound at precise intervals but confined to a single tone, simplifying every desire and state of mind into an elemental monotone, the tolling evoked in me the awesomeness of a peal of thunder you hear on a summer evening when it wakes you from a dream, the mystery of train wheels rumbling through the deep of the night.

'A nun must have died.'

When the bell was tolling like this we thought it meant a nun was passing peacefully into the next world.

Across the railroad tracks a black stream spewed from the smokestack of the flour mill, surging into the sky above the war-ravaged city like dust rising from a battlefield.

The intense bombardment from the warships during the landing operation would long be remembered in the history of warfare, the grownups liked to say. Pretty much the only structures left intact were the old timber-frame houses in our neighbourhood, which had been seized from the Japanese at the end of the Pacific War, and the two-storey houses on the hill in Chinatown.

While sunlight lingered in the western part of the city, Chinatown was saturated with darkness, as if the smoke were smothering it or else the dust carried by the north wind from the coal yard was settling there like ash. Here at the highest point of the city we had a commanding view of Chinatown and the coloured blankets and lace underwear on the balconies of the sooty houses seized from the Japanese. These were the scenes, the under-side, the mysterious smile of this city. Part of me would always be weighed down by these images. To me, China-town and my neighbourhood were the flooded stern of a listing ship about to sink.

Torches, lit too early in the evening, flared at the public playing field in the eastern part of the city. Framed by the last traces of sunlight the flames swayed and flick-ered in the remnants of the wind. A crowd was crying out, 'Czechoslovakia go home! Poland go home! Puppet regimes go home!' For the entire summer one member from each household had to report to the playing field at sunset to join the slogan-shouting, foot-stamping throng. Grandmother would return from these rallies complain-ing of pain in her lower back and groan all night.

One morning during assembly our principal explained the reason for the protests. Czechoslovakia and Poland, satellites of the Soviet Union, had forsworn their obliga-tions as members of the neutral-nations peacekeeping force by attempting to uncover UN military secrets to pass on to the communist side.

If I buried my head between my knees the outcry from the playing field became a distant hum, kind of like the sound I could make blowing across the narrow mouth of an empty bottle. A sound I associated with the earth groaning deep below the surface, a faint ripple foreshadowing a tidal wave, a lingering breeze licking the roofs of houses.

At home I found Mother retching beside the drain in the yard. For the first time I empathized with the brutish life that women had to live. There was something pathetic and harrowing about Mother's nausea, and this symptom of her pregnancy made me plead silently with her to produce no more brothers and sisters for me. I was afraid she would die if she gave birth again.

I couldn't get to sleep until well into the night. My older sister had bound her emerging breasts with a waistband Grandmother tore from a skirt, and because they were sensitive even to the touch of the sheets, she was tossing and turning and moaning, hands crossed over her chest. Lying awake I tried to count the number of times the night guards tapped their sticks together to signal their approach and the number of wheels on the freight trains that passed by. At daybreak I went back to the pier. The dead cat was nowhere to be seen among the garbage and rotting fish washing up against the embankment, nor was it beneath an abandoned boat I spotted drifting a short distance offshore. Perhaps by now some children in a distant port were dragging its shapeless body around at the end of a pole.

Autumn drew near but the bedbugs, smelling like raw beans, flourished as never before. When the sun shone full on the balcony we took the tatamis outside to dry and scoured the wooden floors of our rooms for the eggs. Though our pyjamas had elastic cuffs, the bedbugs managed to crawl inside, making us itch. The electricity stayed on until midnight and we usually went to sleep with the lights on because they kept the bugs away. But when the lights went out the bugs swarmed out of the tatami straw and the cracks in the floor and launched an all-out attack.

One night when I was half asleep and scratching away at the bugs I was awakened by a *thunk* – it sounded like someone splitting wood. Before I knew it my older brother had thrown on his trousers and shot down the stairs. I could tell from the hubbub on the street that something had happened. My heart quickened and I went out onto the balcony. The electricity was off and it was pitch dark but I could make out the noisy crowd that had filled the street between our house and Ch'iok's. Sliding glass doors scraped open on the balconies above, our neighbours shouting questions to those below. Among the hum of voices the word 'dead' came to my ears like a revelation. The word passed from mouth to mouth like a round, some people shuddering in disgust, others poking their heads through the layers of onlookers. I felt my chin tremble as I looked across the street and saw that the door to Maggie's room was open. The dark-skinned soldier, dressed in an undershirt, was looking down on the street from the balcony, his hands resting on the railing.

I heard the wail of a siren and the next moment an American army jeep arrived. Instantly the crowd parted and there lying in the street was Maggie, drenched in the brightness of the jeep's headlights. Her long, thick hair covered her face and was strewn every which way, like solar flares. 'He threw her into the street,' somebody said.

The man was drunk. The MPs got him into his uniform

and as they loaded him into the jeep, his shirt unbuttoned, he chuckled.

The next day I found Ch'iok giving water to Jennie. The little girl had the hiccups. Ch'iok patiently wiped the moisture trickling from the corner of Jennie's mouth. But no amount of water could stop the hiccups.

'They're going to put her in an orphanage,' Ch'iok said. She sounded a bit sulky, like on the day she told me that Maggie was bound for America in the spring – the dark-skinned soldier had decided to marry her.

Maggie had looked happy then. Once I found her washing his feet as he sat on the edge of the bed. Her dyed hair was piled high on her head and as I stared at the clean nape of her neck she turned to me. Without makeup she looked like she had no eyebrows. She gently beckoned me. 'It's okay. Come on in.'

'Jennie went to the Catholic orphanage,' Ch'iok told me with a fierce scowl two days later. Her eyes were red and puffy. A younger sister of Maggie's had come to pack up the dead woman's belongings. Maggie's room remained empty for some time. But I didn't go up there to do home-work or play with Ch'iok anymore. Instead I called to her from the street on my way to school every morning.

As Mother's stomach continued to swell almost imperceptibly beneath her skirt I grew more and more convinced she wouldn't survive another birth. As it turned out, the one who failed was Grandmother, whose stinging hands and pungent, vicious curses had seemed to make her healthier by the day. One morning she collapsed while doing the laundry. She never recovered. My baby brother, who had practically lived on her back, became my big sister's responsibility.

When Grandmother began needing a bedpan, Mother and Father agreed to move her to the countryside, where Grandfather lived.

'The effects can last twenty years,' Mother whispered to Father. 'That's why they say a stroke can melt a rock.' And in a slightly louder voice, 'When you're old there's only one place to be, and that's next to your husband, whether you love him or hate him.' Finally, in a loud tone, 'We'd better arrange a taxi for her.'

Grandmother was as helpless as a baby. As Ch'iok had done with Jennie, I would go into Grandmother's room when no one else was home and comb her hair and give her water to drink and sometimes I gently checked her nappy.

On the day Grandmother was to leave, Mother dressed her in clean clothes and then reported, 'She still has her figure because she never had children.'

And then Father left with her for the village where Grandfather lived with her younger sister and their children. 'I don't feel right about it,' Father sighed when he returned. He spoke falteringly. 'I don't think they'll be happy with her. She'll be a thorn in their side. You know, it's amazing – I thought she wouldn't know anyone but apparently she recognized your father – she spread open her jacket, took his hand and placed it on her chest. Can you imagine how frustrated she must have been all these years? "Till death do us part" – makes you wonder.'

'There was a lifetime of bitterness inside that woman,' said Mother. 'But didn't I tell you? We did the right thing sending her there.'

Mother decided to open Grandmother's clothing chest – something Grandmother had never let any of us touch. Eagerly we followed the movement of Mother's hands. One by one she removed the neatly folded articles of clothing and placed them on the floor. Out came Father's old long underwear, which Grandmother had hemmed for her own use, and the Japanese-style baggy trousers she had worn around the house, and clothes made from sheer silk and from thick, glossy silk and from other fabrics woven in the traditional way. As Mother continued to reach into the chest for clothing worn perhaps once or twice in a lifetime, I finally realized that Grandmother was not coming back, that the days when she might have worn such clothes were gone, and I felt a chill sweep through the depths of my heart. When had she worn those clothes? And for what special occasion had she stored them deep inside the chest?

The last article of clothing was an otter vest. Mother then groped along the bottom of the chest and produced a tightly wrapped handkerchief. With bated breath we fixed our eyes on Mother's nimble fingers.

With a quizzical expression Mother looked inside the handkerchief. A jade ring broken in two, a tarnished copper belt buckle that looked about to crumble, a few nickel coins from the Japanese occupation, buttons of various sizes that might once have been attached to clothing, some coloured threads – such were the contents.

'Really, Mother!' she clucked. 'Saving broken jade is like saving bits of pottery.' Mother rewrapped the objects and tossed the handkerchief into the empty chest. After setting aside the long underwear and other underclothing to use as rags she moved the remainder of the clothing to her own chest. The otter fur was of high quality, she told us – she would use it as a muffler.

The next day I sneaked into Grandmother's chest and

retrieved the wrapped-up handkerchief and took it to the park, where I walked sixty-five paces from the statue of the general – one step for each year Grandmother had lived. The last step brought me to an alder – the fifth tree into a grove – and there I dug deep and buried the handkerchief and its contents.

Toward the end of winter word arrived that Grandmother had passed on. It was just the previous summer that she had left in the taxi. Mother, now in her ninth month, did something uncharacteristic: she began crying as she caressed Grandmother's clothing chest, which was stuffed topsy-turvy with all of our threadbare clothing.

That evening I hid among the odds and ends in the back room, where no one could find me, and when everyone had gone to bed I went to the park. The sky was black but I found the fifth alder tree without having to count to sixty-five steps.

The damp handkerchief, buried deep in the ground for two seasons, stuck to my palm like rotten straw. I brushed the dirt off the halves of the ring, the tarnished belt buckle, and the coins and held them tenderly. They felt exactly the same. They warmed up in my hand but soon the cold would return.

I replaced the objects in their grave beneath the tree. After I had tamped the dirt down and brushed off my hands I started back toward the statue, taking even steps. At the count of sixty I was there. Hmm – it had been sixty-five steps the previous summer. Did this mean it would be fifty paces next summer? And a year later, or ten years later, would one giant step take me there?

Since it was winter and late at night there was no one to give me a disapproving look if I climbed the statue. So

I clawed my way onto the pedestal and then to the binoculars that the general held against his stomach. From there I looked down on the city with its sprinkling of lights. The cries of the previous summer, swelling like dust from a battlefield, were gone. Now it was still. As I strained to listen to the sounds flowing gently through the darkness I felt as if I were tapping an undiscovered vein of water near the core of the earth.

The sea was a black plane. I drank in the wind that had been blowing all night from the East China Sea, and the seaweed smell it carried. I saw the oblong light framed by the open shutter of the two-storey house on the Chinatown hill and imagined a pale face revealed within it. I felt the soft breath of spring hiding in the chilly air.

Something was budding in my warm blood, something unbearably ticklish.

'Life is . . .' I murmured. But I couldn't find the right word. Was there a single word for today and yesterday, with their jumble of indistinguishable, all too complicated colours, a word to embrace all the tomorrows?

And then it was spring again and I was in Year 6. One day my older brother brought home a puppy. With Grandmother gone, it had the run of the house, messing and shedding anywhere it pleased.

I had grown the better part of a foot in the past twelve months, and last year I'd started using my older sister's Oxford-cloth, rose-embroidered school bag.

All winter long my rat pack and I had sneaked coal from the freight trains and as always had run wild through the streets. Occasionally I had closeted myself in the back room at home to read popular romances and such.

One Saturday afternoon I was on my way home from school – Saturday being the one day when we didn't have classes in the afternoon. 'Tomorrow's worm medicine day, so be sure to skip breakfast,' our teacher had reminded us on Friday. 'The worms won't take the medicine on a full belly.'

There was much less rebuilding in the neighbourhood now, but Corsican weed was still boiled and the smell still seemed to dye the air yellow.

In the simmering yellow sunlight I frequently stopped to spit. 'Feels like the worms are going nuts,' I muttered once again.

I saw Ch'iok mixing permanent-wave solution in a can in the beauty shop at the three-way junction. Her father had lost a leg in a conveyor belt at the flour mill and had moved away with his wife the previous winter. Ch'iok stayed behind and was living with the people who ran the beauty shop. Every day I passed it on my way to and from school and saw her through the glass door. Usually I found her sweeping in between pulling down her small sweater, which constantly rode up her back to reveal her bare waist.

I walked past the beauty shop. The yellow sunlight filling the street looked like thousands of feathers soaring into the air. When was it? Shaking my head in irritation I tried to revive a distant, barely remembered dream. When was it? I continued toward home, and when I arrived I looked at the open window of the two-storey house on the hill. He was leaning partway out of the window, beckoning me.

I started up the hill, drawn as if by a magnet, and he disappeared from the window. A moment later he heaved open the gate to the house and there he was. His broad, sallow face still wore that mysterious smile.

He offered me something wrapped in paper and when I accepted it he went back inside. Through the open gate I saw a narrow, shaded front walk and a yard with so much sun it startled me, sunlight dancing and darting on the translucent skin of his bare feet with every step he took.

At home I went into the back room, locked the door and opened the package. Inside was bread dyed in three colours, the kind the Chinese ate on their holidays, and a thumb-size lantern decorated with a plastic dragon.

I hid these items in a cracked jar that no one used. Mother was in labour in my parents' room, but instead of looking in on her I went upstairs and sneaked into the storage cabinet like I did when playing hide and seek. It was midday but not a ray of light entered my hiding place. As I listened to Mother screaming that she wanted to die I realized the church bell was tolling and then I fell into a sleep that was like death itself.

I learned later that by the time I awoke, Mother had pushed her eighth child into the world after a terrible labour. In the darkness of the cabinet a sense of help-lessness and despair came over me and I called out to her. I felt inside my underwear and finally I understood the humid fever that had been closing about me like a spider web.

My first menstrual flow had begun.

Running Man

'Want to go?'

Ch'aehŭi shook her head, avoiding my gaze. 'Let's just stay here.'

Broken matchsticks lay gathered about her feet. The four walls of the tearoom might as well have vanished, I felt so exposed and insecure. *Stand by me, stand by me!* The imploring voice – Ben E. King? – hovered above the unoccupied tables, gently reverberating among the few patrons before streaming down past their slack legs. To my ears, strange as it may seem, the consistent crying of the melody was primeval. Beneath the table Ch'aehŭi's legs swayed to the steady rhythm. She must have been bored out of her mind – all because of me. Anxious me.

'How many times have we met?' The same stupid question. Instantly I regretted it.

'Twenty? Thirty? Maybe forty?' Her tone was matter-of-fact, no hint of playfulness.

I smirked. She looked up with a *So what?* expression.

We've been seeing each other almost every week, she the just-turned-21-year-old niece of a colonel, and I the colonel's driver. *Snap crack* – another matchstick bites the dust. This was our routine, parked for the day at a tearoom over a cup of bitter coffee and the occasional complimentary serving of barley tea.

Stand by me. Stand by me. Pretending to focus on the pleading tone of the singer, which aroused no pity in us, grabbing the matchbox and religiously splintering its contents, we managed to kill the better part of a day. And how many such days had we killed? Ten? Thirty? Who knows, maybe seventy? Could I blame her for her mechanical tone? At times I felt compelled to tell her I loved her, especially when we transitioned to drinking late into the night. I would draw close from across the table, my gaze coming to rest on the hand holding the glass at which she sipped, so studious and silent, but then the spectral illusion returned and my mind would whirl and my head would fall to the table. Because her hand resembled his in its pallor and frigidity, a hand so frail but absolutely substantial in its own way, a hand that had yielded the pair of keys in my pocket that obsessed me, a pale white hand that was sucking me into its palm.

'Shall we go?' I asked, my eyes following the movement of her hands.

She didn't respond. Head down, she was absorbed in reducing the matchsticks to splinters. There was a delicate sheen to the hair flowing down the nape of her neck. More than once, returning to the base as the late-evening curfew approached, I had an urge to embrace all of her, from the crown of her black hair to the bare, round soles of her feet as I noted the red warning signs on the barbed-wire fence – 'Intruders Will Be Shot' and 'DANGER' – and watched the barracks come in and out of sight. But her shoulders would tremble and my hands resting on them would slip off. I wondered if it was a reflex – it didn't feel like rejection – but as always the movement left my hands helpless, and my desire turned cold. I realized belatedly that the resistance was not from Ch'aehŭi but from the pair of keys in my pocket.

'Want to go?' This time more forcefully.

She brushed off her skirt and rose.

Down the steep stairs we went, the wooden steps creaking feebly. At the landing our ankles were bathed in sunlight. She squinted and frowned, as if blinded by the light. Her eyes were bloodshot. She must have been tired.

'Where to?' I mumbled. It was high noon, its arrival feeling oppressively sudden.

'I'm just going to go home,' she said, pressing a hand against her temple.

What could I say? It made perfect sense, played out as she looked.

Infused with sunlight and lurking arrogantly, the street was like a river I had to swim across.

Before I knew it she had strayed off toward the bus stop.

'Why don't you take a cab?'

I caught up with her and she came to a stop.

A taxi pulled over. I ushered her in and reached into my pocket for the fare. My hand felt paper money and then the two small, hard metal objects and instantly tensed. Two pairs of eyes gazed at me dubiously.

'What is it?' she said.

I thought she was going to get out. Embarrassed, I gave her a *no problem* wave of the hand. 'No, it's nothing.'

'All right then!' She yanked the door shut and off went the taxi.

Hands in my pockets, I decided I would walk as slowly as possible. Three months ago, the package containing the keys had been delivered to me at the base. The moment I cleared the layers of wrapping and took them in hand, they began glittering as if they'd come alive. And then it hit me – he must have died. I should have left then and there to confirm it. Instead of taking hold of Ch'aehŭi's shoulders and hitting on her with nonsense like 'Let's go somewhere high and sing to the heavens', I should have gone looking for him, should have found him lying on his side on the sandy beach or wearing a goofy, seductive smile in the secluded woods. I should have spread open his hardened hands and closed my fingers around his death. Instead I held Ch'aehŭi and without realizing it babbled to her what he used to say to me.

He was noticeably unstable around the time I walked out on him. He was penetrating me more deeply, his manhood and mine persisting in their illicit union.

'I don't write to my mother anymore.' He used to say this after we finished, when I'd spread open the curtain and was looking down at the ground. It was a casual remark but I quickly unpacked the meaning. By then his eyes were fretful and his drooling lust had dissipated. His mounting instability told me he was becoming more reliant on me. When we were drinking he would fall apart, resting his head against my shoulder and weeping.

'Chŏngsu-ya,' he would tell me, 'let's go somewhere high up!'

It was the season when trees course with sap. The tender leaves glittered as if to dispel the nightfall, and I lured him deeper into the dark woods. 'No, we shouldn't,' he retorted in a muffled voice, sobbing and pounding his chest. 'Why not go out with a girl?' I used to tell him. 'There have to be some girls you fancy at school.' His eyes would lock onto mine. 'You're mocking me. You're having fun at my expense.'

By then I had begun my furtive betrayal of him,

39

running off to do my military service and attempting to free myself of the grip of his white hand. And now he was dead and gone, leaving me a pair of keys. I couldn't figure out why he went to so much trouble to locate the person who had abandoned him, then resort to mailing him the keys. Those keys now clung to me righteously, thwarting me and defeating my attempts at reasoning. They had become an indecipherable code, and I had been reduced to a state of suspended animation.

The blaring of a horn brought me to a halt. I caught a glimpse of blue sky that was erased the next moment by a bus and the baleful expression of the driver staring down at me. I had strayed off the pavement and into the street and was caged in by vehicles, the throng of occupants shooting me looks through open windows. Flustered, I crept back to the pavement. And now the bus driver was screaming his head off. I couldn't hear him above the cacophony of honking, but almost broke out laughing when I imagined the hackneyed curses – *Crazy son of a bitch! You got a death wish? You're out of your mind!*

The sun was high in the sky. Would midday last forever? Here I was, a lunatic in the sun's orbit. Exhaustion came over me – the stream of vehicles; the throng of pedestrians bumping shoulders, the noise filtering among them, their snooty or else indifferent gazes; high noon at an eternal zenith; and inside my pocket a three-day pass containing more time than I could ever hope to kill. Again I focused on trudging as slowly as I could.

Yesterday my three-day furlough came through. I had to resolve the collision between the three-month reign of the pair of keys and my declaration that I would no longer put my life on hold. The keys had rendered me hamster-like on a treadmill that always came to a stop at the conclusion that I had to keep them. Did owning the keys mean owning his death? Thanks to this edifice of thoughts, when the sergeant handed me the pass and said, 'Have a good time!' I was able to respond to his jest with a quip of my own – 'Yes sir, I'm off on my honeymoon!' I was still in deferment mode on this the first day of my furlough. I had called Ch'aehŭi and wasted half the day at the tearoom and now was fixing to desert the remaining hours of it. But time had sunk its teeth into me and wouldn't let go. I took the keys from my pocket and placed them in my palm. Clammy with perspiration, they remained lifeless in the sunlight, mere metal pieces. Back they went to my pocket, and off I went again. 'What am I afraid of?' I mumbled. The answer brought me to a halt. Blinded by the sunlight, I brought my fingertips together against my forehead to shade my eyes, and I surveyed the surroundings – which way to his place?

He had rented an apartment in an old wooden structure along the river. It had been a while since I visited him for the last time, but the building looked the same. Indigence and filth were everywhere. The alley was narrow and muddy and life held onto it with germ-like tenacity. The harsh voices of women shot forth from every open window, and a flock of naked kids roamed around. The clamour of crying children and the shouting of the womenfolk beating them filled the alley. Was anything tolerated apart from the craving for food and sex? The stench of day-to-day life issued from every nook of the building. Not even a typhoon could wash away the scum. I always felt that time had come to a standstill here – and yet children continued to be born and raised.

His unit was at the far end of the second floor. I started up the stairs. The wooden steps looked thinner and kept creaking despite my attempt to tread softly. I used to experience a kind of terror during my Sunday afternoon visits. The creak produced by the sole of my shoe would reach my brain before my next footfall, making me believe the sound was coming instead from my head, proof of my imminent breakdown. And if I tried to arrive at step two before step one creaked, my creaking brain would crack and my life would be crushed into granules and rain down on me. I would arrive at his door practically crawling and drained of energy.

His door was shut tight and locked. But when I took the keys from my pocket and inserted the room key, the lock opened with a cheerful click. The sound of metal meeting metal was all the more unreal among the continuing shouts of the women beating their children.

The interior was in disarray, as if he had left in a hurry on a trip. I briefly fancied him popping out with a naughty grin from the piles of clothing or the crumpled bedsheets. He didn't, of course, but with every step I raised a puff of thick dust, which I took to be the settling of his breath. Sunlight filtered through the haze. I opened the window and the dusty sediment of his existence came alive, as if revived by his breath. I began to comb through his living space. I turned the wastebasket upside down; it yielded only cigarette butts and ash. On the desk was a fountain pen and its holder and a bottle of dried ink. But I saw no writing. And now I had the impression that he had stepped out somewhere nearby.

An open book at the head of his bed caught my eye. I picked it up and it released a puff of dust. I pored over the printed page:

> *A lion has come out from his lair,*
> *the destroyer of nations;*
> *he has struck his tents, he has broken camp,*
> *to harry your land*
> *and lay your cities waste and unpeopled.*
> *Well may you put on sackcloth,*
> *beat the breast and wail,*
> *for the anger of the Lord*
> *is not averted from us.*

The Book of the Prophet Jeremiah. I lost interest and tossed it to the floor; specks of dust shot from between the pages. That he was reading the Bible was a revelation, but I found it distasteful.

I failed to discover any clue to his whereabouts. Feeling burned out, I perched myself on the edge of the bed and swept the room with my eyes.

Ah! Why didn't I see that? The tiny keyhole in his desk drawer – how cute. I produced the other key and was about to insert it when I flinched. My fingers tingled with dread – what if his white hand was waiting in the drawer to clutch me even more tightly? I retreated a step and dithered. And then was struck by a fierce impulse to leave the apartment as it was, lock the door, and go. But in the next moment: *What a stupid idea! He's dead, remember?* And then I admonished the hand that held the key to the drawer: *Come on, don't be a coward.* But I just couldn't insert it. *Let's hold off a little, till I feel better.* I returned to

43

the bed and lay down on my stomach. But I couldn't stand the sun, so I got up, staggered to the window, and drew the curtain, and while doing so managed to tear off a corner, allowing a triangular patch of sunlight to remain on the floor. The women's harsh voices and the children's sharp screeching penetrated the walls and floor so clearly I felt I could almost take hold of them. I buried my face in the bed. I had once asked him why he lived with such godawful noise – why couldn't he move somewhere quiet? His answer was 'Well . . .' followed by an ambiguous smile. The noise from downstairs and next door gradually dulled into something more malleable, more soft and fuzzy, and then to a hum that finally died out.

I opened my eyes, not to the pink globe of the rising sun but to the advance of night, awakened by a sensation of my tonsils swelling uncontrollably, accompanied by memories of a bewildering pain whose form and intensity I couldn't gauge. Such an experience was not new: from time to time, on my hard cot in the barracks, I would awaken from a dream in which my shirt collar was tightening around my neck or my jacket was ripping open at the seams.

It was the dead of night, but the moon lit up the grid of the window frame. Intermittent periods of darkness followed, which I marked up to the clouds. There was the occasional flash of light from the carbide lamps used by the fishermen on the river. I rose, went to the window and opened it, but saw only darkness lurking below. The memory of my painful, uneasy dreams of seams ripping resurfaced until I felt it was the seams of my mind that were tearing. I reached out in despair for the darkness, but it slipped through my fingers. I took the keys from my pocket. They still had the spark of life. But the chaotic, amorphous anxiety that filled the room was thrusting me off. I turned on the light and suddenly all was exposed. And that's when it finally sank in that I was in his room, that I had unlocked the door, that I was now fully involved. I regarded the desk drawer lock without faltering and inserted the key with a steady hand, and the drawer opened without a fuss.

His past opened for me as well. I came face to face with a gloomy, depressed boy and his mother with her hair in a neat bun and her eyes gleaming coldly inside her spectacles. The kimono suited this woman who had abandoned her son. She had ditched him before he had turned one to re-marry, this time to a Japanese man, and had sent an ample monthly stipend along with a letter beginning with a shameless *My dear darling son*. In this desk drawer of secrets she had grown younger by the day while absorbing the arrows of love and hatred shot by the son who wouldn't otherwise have remembered the face of a mother who had the eerie beauty of a poisonous mushroom.

I gently closed the drawer containing this brief yet complicated fragment of his life. There was nothing about his death, nothing about me, nothing even about the pair of keys. How ludicrous was my idea of taking ownership of his death. Couldn't I be unmoored from those damned keys? And from his pale white hand and the memories that clung to it? I returned to the window, feeling I was about to explode. The dense darkness held firm. I took a deep breath. And another, and another, and yet another. But the air held no refreshment. Again I drank, inhaling the darkness, until I felt it clogging my lungs. I yearned for daybreak and an end to the thick wall of night.

At sunrise I jumped out of bed, bolted outside and called Ch'aehŭi. 'Ch'aehŭi-ya, let's go somewhere we've never been and get off the train and go our separate ways like a couple of strangers, then bump into each other – what do you think?'

Two days of furlough remained and I had to come up with something. And so we parked ourselves in the corner of the tearoom and schemed while waiting for our order.

Ch'aehŭi was like a little girl, jittering with excitement. 'This is fantastic, a special outing. We'll be in a time-capsule, we'll end up somewhere in the past or else in the future!'

Off we went, each with a ticket in hand, our destination somewhere in the past or the future. But no matter how we recited the names of the small city and the station we had chosen, they came out sounding foreign, and our desperate performance began with a mood of constant waiting. Out she came from the station and strutted toward me like a big boy. I pretended not to notice her in her yellow dress as she passed by me with a faint smile on her flushed face.

What I saw through the train windows was commonplace but awkward and blurred, looking more like shadow than substance. Arriving at our destination, I saw streets simmering amid the din, their grime exaggerated and countrified. Ch'aehŭi alone was refreshing to my eyes; I imagined her in the embrace of a strong wind and kept my eyes glued to her. The main street held a weekly market. For half the day her yellow dress caught my eye. We must have passed each other umpteen times. She walked sometimes upright, seemingly immersed in surroundings that looked ordinary to me, but other times she meandered stealthily with a deflated expression. I plodded along thinking of the meaninglessness of it all. How was it that the play-acting I had suggested – a pair of strangers in an unfamiliar place meeting fortuitously and starting anew – could only end in fatigue and trouble? How much longer would I follow her? There was no way I could run up and pretend to bump into her. The street was too peaceful for that to happen, tedious like stagnant water, and besides, she and I lacked the pathos that would have lent reality to such an encounter.

The sunlight was dispersing, the market was closing and the main street was raucous with the departing vendors and peddlers. I thought I glimpsed her among the throng, but that was the last I saw of her. Our rendezvous never materialized; our play was a flop. Assuming she had already left, I wandered off.

I struck out for the train station as night descended. Along the way I saw what I took to be a group of mourners returning from a funeral. The women and children following the empty bier were silent and appeared to have come to a standstill, bringing the procession to a halt. I stopped as well. The procession was etched in darkness, the ground looking denser and softer in the gloom. But then a breeze stirred this tableau and I realized the procession was actually moving, but ever so slowly and silently. I caught a whiff of dead skin and watched until the mourners had passed in front of me. Then I realized why the procession had evoked in me such feelings of sorrow and yet menace the moment I registered it – it reminded me of him. And now the surroundings were no longer unfamiliar. I was back in the past, recalled to it by a complete and utterly intact memory – the day I first met him, the day he imprinted himself in my mind.

'MynameisCh'unhyangI'meighteenyearsofage,myname isCh'unhyangI'meighteenyearsofage,mynameis . . .'

'Hey.' He extended his hand. It was fair like a girl's. *Come on*, the hand seemed to be telling me.

'MynameisCh'unhyangI'meighteenyearsofage,todayis Buddha'sBirthdaytheeighthdayofApril,todayisBuddah's BirthdaytheeighthdayofApril.'

The girls were dancing in a circle around a pagoda. They kept a steady rhythm as they repeated the flood of syllables. Their circle dance would not stop, nor would the recitation that whirled up and around the top of the thirteen-storey stone pagoda, holding it hostage. Screaming their recitation, the ties of their traditional costumes fluttering, the girls looked like *mudang*, practitioners of our native spirituality. It was almost sunset, and their ritual made sorrow seep from every recess of the park. I was bound by the sound and seized with fright. I offered my hand and the next moment his pale hand was clutching my fingers. That cold, frail-looking hand glued mine to it and I was pulled up from the bench.

'Looklookit'sstillit'sstill,it'sturnedcross-eyedit'sstill.' Behind us the girls' ringing voices.

'It's a kind of hypnosis game,' he explained without looking back.

I followed him down countless alleys, then across several junctions.

He was right behind me as we came to his door, and he shoved me inside. He unbuttoned my clothing, and I could tell he had done this before. And then he was naked. He was a man of few words. All he said afterwards as I lay stretched out on my stomach was, 'How about washing up.' The air was dead still. I lifted enough of the curtain to peek outside. I saw an untended garden with a clump of lacklustre cosmos. 'Are they fading already?' he asked in an impassive tone. I closed the curtain and turned back to him without answering. 'It was awfully windy last night.' He displayed no interest in this remark of his, no anticipation of how I might react to it. Before I knew it my eyes were following the purple smoke rising from the cigarette between the fingers of his pale hand. It was the only movement in the room. The thin plume of smoke expanded into boundaries of the still space.

'Question – what goes up into the sky with its hair all messed up?' I asked.

'Smoke!' he answered at once.

What a lame riddle. But now both his gaze and mine were following the smoke.

And that was my first encounter with him.

Why were we always such sad sacks during my afternoon visits? In my distorted mind's eye I saw a pair of dried fish sweating incessantly and panting with lust, against a background of sunlight falling like flakes of dry skin against a closed curtain, and cosmos blossoms in a wasted lot.

★

I tried again to get Ch'aehŭi to go somewhere we had never been.

'I'd rather be stuck in a movie theatre.' She smirked. 'It's no use, you know. I was so worn out on my way home. All I was thinking was, why are we so boring that we have to put on this idiotic act?'

I knew she wouldn't go, but I bought myself a train ticket anyway, went to a city I'd never been to, and spent half a day looking for her. Of course she was nowhere to be seen. I slunk around like a stray dog. This city was larger than the previous one and its streets were well paved. I walked nonstop but with no interest in what I saw and heard. I was expecting freedom and comfort in this anonymous environment, but found neither. My legs were getting sore. Across the street was a tearoom; I dashed inside.

I ordered coffee and looked out of the barred window, wiping my hands with the damp towel offered by the server. The second-floor location offered a view of the building across the street. What kind of building was it? Suddenly a mob of blue uniforms rushed out from behind it and onto an expanse of open ground. *What the —?* The server brought my coffee and followed my gaze out of the window. 'Reservists,' she mumbled before returning to the counter. My eyes remained on the field. The blue uniforms somehow looked soiled yet full of vitality.

'Left! Right! Down on your stomach!' Familiar words every day at the base but sounding so unfamiliar off the base. The men moved precisely, then broke into a run, their boots raising dust. They disappeared behind the building. I shot to my feet, my eyes following them, but lost my balance. At the next moment I felt as if I was being ejected through the window – then *bang*, I hit the window bar. Hand on my forehead, I plopped back down. But I still felt gravity-free, as if catapulted into space. A thought sparked – it was the last day of my furlough and I had to return to the base. And then from behind the building came blue sparks running toward me. I felt dizzy but didn't look away.

It was all so dreamlike. I saw a very dark and narrow place. But it promised abundant warmth and eternal comfort, and I entered feeling like a beam of light. I was relieved, totally protected. I opened my eyes. It was dark. Sure enough, here I was in his bed. I turned on the light. But why was I still here? I went outside. The shops were closed and I wondered what time it was. An exciting thought struck me. I found a still-open pharmacy, but the proprietor was about to pull the metal shutter down over the entrance. I told him I needed to make a phone call. He pointed to a pay phone. My hands were trembling and I was barely able to dial the number.

'Hello?' A man's subdued voice.

I asked for Ch'aehŭi and heard the man summon her several times in between the words of the national anthem, which told me television programming was ending for the night.

'Hello.' Her voice sounded far off.

'It's me, Chŏngsu.' I realized I was panting.

'What's going on? Did something happen?'

'Can you have a baby with me?'

Silence.

'You know, a baby, with me.' I was still panting.

'No, I don't want that.' Her voice was calm, the tone dry. And then she hung up.

'Is there something you need, sir?' The proprietor's voice was mixed with the coins pouring out of the phone, which he was emptying for the night.

I shook my head.

'It's closing time,' he said.

Back out on the street I heard the coins clinking and then the shutter hitting the ground. No light leaked from the shop; it was pitch dark. I felt peaceful. The darkness seemed strangely clear, and I felt I could see angels. I opened my eyes wider. The darkness breathed silently. But I knew there was a new pain forcing its way toward me. I started running. My feet bounced off the glossy asphalt pavement.

The more I ran the lighter I felt. The wind slashed at my face. How powerless was a pair of keys in this lucid, infinite darkness. I took them from my pocket and tossed them as far as I could. I didn't wait to hear them hit the ground. I would never return there.

I was running for my life, and as I ran I saw a hazy mist ease toward me around a bend.

Mermaid

Look at her! Marvelling at Sunyŏng shelling and devouring a string of boiled chestnuts, I think back to my husband's nonchalant acquiescence in my plan to celebrate the girl's twelfth birthday with a mother–daughter overnight trip, and my gushing turns quickly to venting: a man who gets jittery when the girl goes on a day trip suddenly turns into Mr Generosity?

'I hope you won't mind if I take Sunyŏng to the beach? It's her birthday.' I had hoped he would catch my implication that she wouldn't be eager to go anywhere with her mother once she moved up to middle school.

'Why not?' was his answer. 'And I can take Up'yŏng fishing.'

Hearing this, our third-year middle-school son, who has developed a shadow of a moustache and is noticeably more taciturn, bolted down the rest of his dinner and made a silent exit to his room.

Hmm, a tacit father–son scheme. My curiosity was piqued. I couldn't blame my hypersensitivity. Rather, I was suspicious: these days the boy was acting much more mature than his age, as if he'd already flown the nest. Until last year he would give Sunyŏng a daily rap on the head, driving her to tears, for going through his things. But now he wallows, gazing with pity at her – though in all fairness his expression is more complicated than that – when she blabbers nonstop next to him at the dinner table or sings along with the television. A gaze that sets my heart trembling.

Our trip happens to fall on a holiday weekend. I imagine my husband packing up the fishing gear with Up'yŏng. Lustrous autumn sunlight streams through the windows of the bus and glistens on Sunyŏng's hair. At the slightest movement of her head the rays disperse into a prism of colours – yellow, red and violet – that hurt my eyes. The light weaves its way through her sparse, silk-skein hair and comes to rest on the milk-white part.

'This is so gross!' She brushes the chestnut husks and crumbs from her clothing onto the handkerchief over her lap. 'Like a bunch of bugs!'

'Look at those leaves!' My eyes dart to the hills. 'The colours are so brilliant already!' The profusion of red foliage overwhelms the surroundings.

She's not impressed. 'How much longer do we have to go?'

'Two more hours.'

'I'm bored to death.' She squirms and yawns.

'How about a nice nap? I'll wake you up when we get there. And your tummy's all right? No travel sickness?'

Instead of answering she turns her back to me. 'Would you undo it – please!'

The bra. *Come on, you're not a baby anymore!* Silently chiding her, I slide my hands under her blouse and unhook it.

'Ahh.' She heaves a sigh of relief. 'I was suffocating!' She slumps back in her seat. Just for fun I had bought her first bra for her budding chest. It must have been pinching her.

'You're not sleepy? Then look – there's so much to see!'

A herd of black goats graze on a gentle slope. The herder boy waves at the bus. The sunlight falling on the withering grass looks so soft.

The bus makes a brief stop in the next town. At the station a gaggle of women are hawking *mŏru* in wooden basins, and Sunyŏng has to have some. I shudder at the sight of the wild grapes, imagining their sour taste, but slip a few bills through the open window next to the girl and obtain a bunch for her just before the bus pulls out. Sunyŏng spreads her handkerchief over her lap and starts in on the fruit. I watch, bemused, as she munches and then with a napkin scrupulously dabs at the inky juice around her mouth. Her fuzzy round cheeks look like a pair of peaches. My heart feels leaden as I gaze at her innocent face – does she have any inkling of what this trip could mean?

I am a zealot of moderation and common sense, and I impress on the kids that these are life's foremost virtues. And yet from the start of this trip I have caved in to her unbridled and incessant demands – though not from a lapse of responsibility or from anticipating two days of freedom.

Already I'm dreading our return trip, and especially the changes in her views on life and the world. How cruel will that be? These thoughts have left me feeling like a malefactor, scolding myself for feeling sentimental and grief-stricken – this might be our last trip together.

Announcing our mother–daughter excursion, I had asked where she would like to go. 'The ocean!' she shouted. 'I'm excited!'

My husband had reluctantly butted in. 'The ocean is better in summer, don't you think? Why now, when it'll be cold and dreary? How about a hot spring instead?'

'I've never seen the ocean,' she pouted. 'Daddy's gone ocean fishing with Bro, so it's my turn with Mummy.'

Hmm, true enough. My husband grimaced. An ocean beach was where Sunyŏng had been abandoned.

Having decided to adopt a baby girl from the orphanage, we had cautiously inquired about her birth.

'We don't have much to go on,' said the administrator. 'She wasn't put up for adoption. Someone found her at a beach on the East Sea. It's a tourist spot, but visitors are scarce in the winter. . . Heartless parents – they must have hoped she'd be carried out to sea.'

Not once have we ventured to the seaside with Sunyŏng. We have plenty of excuses – she's too young, there are too many bugs, it's not the right season, the list goes on. We've never admitted it to each other but we know all too well the real reason – her abandonment there, combined perhaps with our trepidation at the possible emergence of memories of an ocean beach, dormant ever since she was a three-month-old baby. Instinctively we avoid the sea.

Overlooking my husband's pique, I had him reserve two express bus tickets to a tourist town on the East Sea. Again I asked myself if that made me a partner in crime. For the trip I prepared a whole new wardrobe for her – underwear, nightwear, even a nice, dressy coat. This was contrary to my mantra that she who handles an unusual event coolly handles it most wisely. Perhaps I had already given in to the worst-case scenario: that this would be Sunyŏng's farewell trip.

And now she's asleep against my shoulder. I reposition her head and gather her spilling hair, which reeks of shampoo. I always remind her to rinse thoroughly but she tends to rush the process.

Dare I expect our relationship will be the same once she finds out I'm not her birth mother, given the occasional feelings of dislike and betrayal between us until now? Affection, hatred and hostility tend to permeate family affairs, and I fear there will be discord among the four of us, and that Sunyŏng and I will have difficulty accepting the existential scepticism she would experience at much too early an age. Even so, my husband and I agree that she needs to know the truth before she gets older and finds out from someone else. No secret is sealed forever, but we want to at least prevent her from experiencing humiliation and shame from a second-hand source.

The bus chugs over a high pass and down a narrow ridge to join the coastal road. The autumn sun is already setting. I gently nudge her awake.

'The ocean – it's really the ocean!' Eying the darkening sea with no trace of drowsiness, she lets out a strident cheer. 'I can smell it. I want to run down the beach in my bare feet!' She's jiggling up and down.

I place a hand on her shoulder. 'Hush!' Concealing my anxiety at the jolt of vigour in her voice, I tell her to stop fussing. 'Can't you wait a bit? We'll be there soon.'

Peeved by the unexpected scolding, she is briefly sullen, but begins chattering as soon as we're deposited on the empty beach. 'Mummy, I love it! But this doesn't feel like the first time, I think I've been here before. And the smell, it's so familiar . . .'

'I don't think so – maybe you got that from a movie or a book?'

I strike out for the beachside inns. The foggy zephyr from the sea dampens our clothing. I see no footprints, and the inns look deserted. Sand in my shoes, I head for a building bearing the sign 'Seaside Hotel', beyond a small pine grove. Sunyŏng gripes that the trees are blocking the beach, but I see no other accommodations that are open for business. I opt for a room on the third floor, offering a better view of the ocean. Most of the other rooms must be vacant, it's so quiet. Our steps echoing in the long corridor sound bleak and desolate.

'Mummy, hurry up. Let's go to the beach!'

'Aren't you tired?' I undo the buttons of her coat. 'I am. We still have time. Let's change first and catch our breath. The sea's not going to run away from us.'

I sit at the vanity and begin removing my makeup with cleansing cream. In the mirror I see her undressing and slipping into a comfortable outfit, then poking around the room – this is her first time at a hotel.

I hear a door open and then a shout: 'Mummy, we have a real bathroom!'

'All hotels have bathrooms.'

Our room sports brightly coloured blankets on the beds, a lamp with a nice shade and a television set. Otherwise it's old and shabby, with a water stain in a corner of the ceiling and dark, mildewed wallpaper behind the vanity. This isn't much of a hotel. But Sunyŏng is at an age where everything away from home looks marvellous and splendid. Outside, dusk is setting in. The sea is in full view beyond the pines, and the waves crashing ashore sound as if they're right below us. I turn on the light and the image of the sea vanishes from the window. That it's now hidden from Sunyŏng's eyes inexplicably sets me at ease. I take my time cleaning my face, then call the front desk.

'Do we have hot water all day? And is the restaurant open?'

'Yes,' says a man. 'You can take a bath any time you wish. And the restaurant is open till ten. It's on the ground floor, next to the lobby.'

I end the call. 'How about a bath? Then we can go down for dinner.'

'All right, Mummy. And after dinner we can go out to the beach.'

I fill the tub with warm water and plop the naked little girl in. She splashes around, cackling. I collect her scattered clothing and hang it in the closet. And I hear her high-pitched voice, punctuated by the sloshing of water:

> 'Soaking my hands in the blue-green sea,
> Soaking my hands in the blue-green sea . . .'

She's been singing on the toilet from a very young age. Up'yŏng and I used to look at each other and giggle, knowing she wouldn't emerge until a few songs later.

Her piping voice muffles the crashing of the waves but I close the curtain anyway. I know I'm at the end of my rope, wanting to block the ocean from her sight even though I've given in to her wish to come here. Such is the angst of delay.

The original plan was for me to make the trip last year. But I've been deferring. My husband too. We lack courage. We seek the perfect time to inoculate her but find plenty of excuses to put it off – she's too young, she's not feeling well, she's been hurt enough already. Pretext, all of it. The root cause is our lack of confidence in our affection for her. *I'm not your birth mother* to her means *You're not my birth daughter* to me – a force powerful enough to thwart a deeper family relationship, and perhaps to leave Sunyŏng feeling betrayed and defenceless. But last spring she had her first period and began seeing her cousins more frequently. How much longer could I put it off? The sharing of secrets is indispensable among girls, and the sharing is unimaginably clandestine. I worry that her girl cousins could be the vehicle for adult whispers to reach her ears.

'When your parents died you needed someone to take care of you, and we wanted a pretty daughter. And we've learned from raising you that sharing a bloodline is not so crucial; what's most important is bonding with one another. I'm always grateful for the higher love that brought you to me.' I've recited these words to myself ever since I decided to reveal to her the circumstances of her birth. But do I really mean them?

How many times did I question whether I truly loved her as I gazed at her while she slept or soothed her when she cried, her face hideously contorted? Try though I might while racked constantly with guilt, I couldn't erase the foreignness I felt, my resistance to this baby that was not of my womb.

Now and then I was tormented by the thought that I never dreamed of raising a child. I believe a person matures from both love and pain, and yet I've never wanted Sunyŏng to be possessed of a special talent or personality. I hoped rather that she would grow up to be an average woman satisfied with nice clothing, a well-stocked kitchen and a well-to-do life. I hoped also that she would become a healthy, self-healing person who wouldn't submerge herself in long-term grief, who would be quick to get back on her feet and dust herself off and compromise with reality. Doing so would lay the foundation for accepting that I am not her birth mother. But how could I hope she would accept this knowledge and take it in her stride without a long period of soul-searching and setbacks?

While raising her I tried to narrow the age gap between us by reliving my own life from age five to nine. My husband felt the foreignness of Sunyŏng as well.

A year after I gave birth to Up'yŏng I was diagnosed with cervical cancer and had my uterus removed. It was my husband – ever the reputable medical practitioner with handsome earnings – who then sounded me out about adoption. I felt a vague sense of responsibility for the education and the good life I'm blessed with, and so his proposal made good sense to me.

Her nightly squalling, starting on her first day with us, lasted a year. She would appear to be drifting off to sleep but then would sit up bawling. She was neither sick nor startled. No amount of cuddling and pacifying would calm her, and we never did learn the cause of her colic. The crying, her face puckered and her hands thrashing, was for us full of derision – it scoffed at the pride we felt deep down inside for raising an abandoned being, it negated our goodwill toward a trusting world, it dismissed what we surely believed to be the love in our hearts.

My husband has never been a patient man. Before three months had passed, he was shuddering in disgust and eying me obliquely. 'It's a nasty habit! What the hell is her problem?' Long after the nocturnal colic was gone, he harboured hate and regret for having adopted her.

I wait for her to finish her bath and down we go to the restaurant. It's as desolate as the guest quarters; we're the only ones there. The sea outside the windows is indistinguishable in the darkness.

She dips a slice of raw fish in the vinegary *koch'ujang*. 'Let's go out to the beach after we eat.' Her eyes stare at the dark expanse.

'Your hair's still wet,' I tell her. 'You'll catch a cold. And it's too late now. How about getting up early so we can watch the sunrise?'

She nods and her begging ends. As we sip our after-dinner hot drinks – coffee for me and cocoa for her – my mind is unquiet: we have to return home tomorrow. When, where and how will I bring it up? Out on the beach where she's dying to go, blurting it in the dark when we can't see each other's face? Will she accept it as casually as she does the sound of the waves?

'I wonder what Daddy and Bro are doing?' she says with a beaming smile.

'I wonder. Maybe tickling each other in their sleeping bag? Or boiling up some ramen? You miss them already?'

'Sure – we're a family! We had breakfast together this morning, and now we're apart. Isn't that weird?'

Oh sweetie, how far apart will we be tomorrow morning? Again I flare up at my husband for leaving me with this burden and going on his merry way. 'That's right, we're a family,' I say with a sigh.

Back in our room she changes into her sleeping gown and slips into bed. But weary as she is, she can't get to sleep in this new setting.

'I feel like a princess, Mummy.' Her face is happy and drowsy. I think of her frilly new sleepwear. 'I'll have a happy dream for sure.'

I give her a smile. Yes, the princess feeling – I too had it at her age. Growing up in poverty with a pack of siblings, how I had longed for my own room with a secret drawer, pretty pyjamas and a bed.

'Happy about what, sweetie?'

'For being really pretty.' And then, counting off on her fingers, 'And for playing awesome piano, living in a cute house and making up with Hyeyŏn.'

Hyeyŏn is her pal who sent her a note after a spat – *This means our friendship is over.* Sunyŏng had showed it to me, gritting her teeth.

'You two are still not talking?'

'She hangs around with the other kids, just to show off. I hate her. Ugyŏng took me home with her and then invited Hyeyŏn so we could make up, but I guess she saw my shoes at the front door and took off. She must really hate me.'

'Don't worry. You'll have more friends in middle school. And maybe Hyeyŏn's just pretending to be mad. Sometimes we act differently from how we feel. And remember, the two of you have been buddy-buddy for a long time. You don't want to get hung up on hatred, otherwise your heart and your face get all ugly.'

'Mummy, you never hated anyone, did you?'

'Me? What makes you think that?'

'Because . . . you're always pretty.'

'Because I'm your mummy, you mean. To me you're always the prettiest girl.' Was this the right moment? 'You know, people tend to—'

But with a loud yawn she buries her head in her pillow saying, 'Daddy and Bro will be cold in the tent. It's so windy!'

'They'll be warm enough in their sleeping bags. . . Should we order some Sprite or something?'

'I already brushed my teeth. You're always talking about rotten teeth—'

'Ah, right! So you're going to bed? Don't want to chit-chat with Mummy?'

'No thank you, I'm sleepy. I want to get up for the sunrise.'

And soon she's dropped off. Perched on my bed, I stare at her roundish face with the small chin, next to the dim lamp. That face doesn't feel familiar, even less so now that she's asleep. How much more can I filter myself into the life of this girl, my daughter, who calls me Mummy?

It's already eleven years since we brought her home. I remember it as if it were yesterday. We decided to celebrate that day, the day we found the foundling, as her birthday. She was a fragile baby with no hair. Her deepest slumber comes when the bulk and mass of those eleven years feel weightless, and then I sink into feelings of helplessness, thinking she inhabits a distant, unattainable land.

Again I murmur to her. 'You needed someone to take care of you, and we wanted a pretty daughter.' Knowing she's far off in slumber-land and can't hear me, I say it louder. Why doesn't my voice sound real? Is what I'm saying true? Did I want a pretty daughter? After I gave birth to Up'yŏng my heart was filled with the boy's exist-ence; I knew then that I had planted in him all my hopes and dreams and had no room for another child. If you have no dreams and hopes for the child you're raising, you've already abandoned that child, haven't you?

The deeper the night, the closer the waves sound. I'm tired but feel sleepless. I fret about returning home tomorrow with the same vague but nervous apprehension still hanging over me.

I pick up the phone intending to order beer from room service. But then she turns over and I hear her shallow breathing. I set the phone down and tiptoe out. It occurs to me that she might wake up and worry about me, but I continue downstairs and then, instead of the restaurant, go out to the beach.

I slip through the ghostly pines and am hit by the violent crash of the waves. The ocean is pitch dark. Only the lapping of water on sand tells me where land and ocean separate. I navigate the beach, keeping clear of the band of white foam. The damp sea breeze permeates my clothing and begins to seep into me. I raise my collar and tuck it around my neck and keep sweeping my hair back. Where exactly was Sunyŏng abandoned, unprotected against the chilly, blustery wind of winter except for the blanket swaddling her? Did the post-partum mother really hope the baby would be washed away without a trace? But identifying the spot and explaining her birth means another abandonment on a soulless beach, doesn't it? Wasn't it true that I longed for Sunyŏng to leave me without a trace, so I could free myself of this heavy burden once and for all? My mind is taxing me.

Suddenly I'm hit with a blast of light. With a silent scream I freeze.

'Who's there?' a man barks.

Blinded by the beam I can only make out two forms.

'Where'd you come from?' The voice is menacing.

'I'm . . . staying at the Seaside Hotel.' I try to grin and imagine myself grimacing awkwardly. 'I just came out for some fresh air!'

'This is a strategic military area.' They study me before lowering the blinding light. 'We're going to ask you to turn back. And it's not safe being out here by yourself – you might run into some thugs.' They resume their patrol.

I bend down and grope around my feet for the fist-size conch revealed by their searchlight. I pick it up and put it to my ear and hear a faint whizzing.

The sound of the soldiers tramping through the surf is muffled by the sand dunes. I turn back toward the way I came. I can't see the lights from the hotel behind the pine grove. Is it really that far? Fright grips the nape of my neck and I break into a sprint. The more pressed I feel to get to the hotel, the deeper my feet sink in the sand. My long, sodden skirt slaps at my knees and then clings to my calves, and I stumble. The lashing of the waves turns into Sunyŏng crying out *Mother!* when she awakens from a nightmare in an empty, unfamiliar room.

Shuddering not just from the chill dampness of the night air, I arrive at our room. The first thing I do is dump her clothing from the closet into the bathtub and turn on the water. As the tub fills I dump her shoes in too. I'm clueless as to why I do this, and not until I'm sure the clothing and shoes are safely submerged do I relax. Sunyŏng breathes gently, dead to the ruckus I've created. I turn off the light, lie flat in my bed and beckon sleep.

At daybreak the next morning I find her bed empty. 'Sweetie, where are you!' I'm terrified. 'In the bathroom?'

No response. I open the bathroom door and see only the wet clothing resembling cast-off skin. I peep outside through the curtain. 'Oh no!' I stifle my scream. There she is in her lacy sleepwear making her way through the pines toward the beach. The long night-dress trailing behind makes it seem as if she is skidding rather than walking.

At the beach she starts running. The gown puffs out like a balloon in the wind. Her footprints, tiny as a bird's, are quickly washed out by the waves.

A newlywed couple, the woman in a green *chŏgori* and red *ch'ima* and the man in a black suit, pass her only to turn and fix her with their gazes.

I can no longer distinguish her white nightdress from the white foam as she romps along. Staring at her as she disappears into the distance, all I can do is scream wretchedly as I call her name, but no sound comes from my mouth.

The Garden Party

Myŏnghye wasn't sure if the gathering darkness had drawn her attention to the clock chiming in the living room, or the other way around; she knew only that it wasn't her habit to focus on each chime of the clock. She was standing on the desk in their spare room papering the ceiling, and when the clock chimed six she climbed down and deposited her tools in the basin.

Before she knew it the shade of evening was surging through their home, except where the open storm window admitted the golden glow of the lingering sunset.

Yunjae, her son, and Myŏnghŭi, her daughter, were sitting on the living room floor, intent on a television show.

'Turn on the light!' she said, fearing they were disappearing slowly into the dusk.

The boy gave her a quick glance, registered his mom's irritation, then rose silently, tiptoed to the wall and flipped the switch.

She stood in place, rotating her head to loosen the stiffness in her neck, drumming her fists against the small of her back, and scanning the floor strewn with newspaper, wallpaper, the paste bucket, and such. Finish up or stop here? The walls were more or less covered but a third of the ceiling remained. If she put if off to the following day she could always soften the paste with water, but setting up all over again would be a pain.

The gathering at the Kims was scheduled for six-thirty.

Even if she hurried the kids to get ready, they'd be lucky to arrive by seven. She wasn't inclined to leave the papering unfinished and venture into the bleakness of early evening with the kids in tow, but it was too late to cancel. Kilmo would be going there straight from the university. For all she knew, he had already arrived and by now the doctor's good wife would have dinner prepared for her and the kids. What would the hostess think if their places at the dinner table went unfilled?

A few days earlier Kilmo had said, 'Guess what – Dr Kim wants us over for dinner. *Us.*' 'Why us?' she had queried. Granted, Dr Kim and Kilmo had gone to the same high school in this small provincial city with its tangled network of family, regional and school ties, a region in which most people knew one another at least in passing, but she still couldn't connect the dots into the kind of relationship that would account for the invitation. Her only clue was the gilded greeting card bearing the name of Dr Kim, president of the alumni association of that prominent high school, that invariably landed in their mailbox early in the new year.

She turned on the light in the guest room to reveal a shower of bouquets issuing from the new wallpaper. The cramped room was in full blossom, but all it made her think of was gaudy makeup.

She imagined Kilmo's response – *What the hell is this? Are you decking out someone's coffin? Or a* mudang *shrine?* Then she recalled the shopkeeper's sour face when he had discovered her picking out a dust-covered roll of flowery wallpaper lying bereft of its plastic wrapping in a corner. He had proceeded to show her a practical, high-end style from one of the sample books. The current

69

trend was for discreet patterns, in fact almost no pattern, he explained. And the fancier the home, the classier the wallpaper. The colours were refined and classic, and she wouldn't have to worry about matching the rolls. And the paper was more durable and held up better to humidity. But the pattern she had found, the scarlet blossoms twice as large as her palms, convinced her, perhaps with the help of a poem she had recalled just then – *a peony blossom falls, and then another.* And when she started in on the work, another possible reason came to mind: nostalgia for the paper she used to see lining the interior of an old chest or an apple crate for temporary clothing storage when she was a girl.

Now as she gazed at the huge, deep red blossoms she could almost hear them drop, one by one. She had zero practical sense, she sighed to herself. Kilmo, meticulous and intolerant of disorder, would surely have it replaced.

Kicking aside the items strewn about the floor, she made a passage to the bathroom, along the way feeling more bits of paste and shreds of newspaper sticking to the soles of her feet with every tiptoed step. She washed her hands then filled a washbasin and while cleaning the paste and paper from her feet she gazed out of the window. The evergreens populating the lower reaches of the left side of the hill behind their home were submerged in thick shadow, whereas the lower reaches to the right – as if in accordance with an ecological plan – were forested with broadleaf trees. And the river enclosing the hill, visible when the leaves had fallen, now looked darker. There was no sign of the white bird tracing an arc in the sky from the river to the pines. It took wing between five and six in the afternoon – a time when she was often seized by ambiguous feelings about life – and drifted through the infinite creep of time suffused with elusive tension, from the still sunlit river to the shade-drenched woods.

She had spotted this bird long ago. On that day she had jotted down in her notebook, *A white bird flew from the river to the woods between five and six.* She kept the little notebook and a pen on the kitchen shelf with the cook-books and kitchen towels, anticipating that what she saw outside, combined with the loneliness and desola-tion she felt between sunset and nightfall, would evoke something powerful within her. The bird's flight must have been much longer that day. She could still recall the image of frosty whiteness that had lingered beyond her casual glance. Her notebook was filled with threads of various feelings: what had caused the acrobat to fall from his rope that day, the one that stretched out of sight over such a vast expanse? Why had that woman lost her mind with no one knowing about it? At the time she must have felt that such jottings were imbued with profound impli-cation, apt metaphor and heightened symbolism, but by now she had forgotten why she was motivated to record them in the first place and they were fading into a mean-ingless code.

She opened the bedroom door. *Damn!* The wardrobe for her dresses was on the far side of the room, and the varnish she'd applied to the floor that morning wasn't yet dry and had the appearance of sticky, glistening toffee. Why hadn't she left her evening wear out? The hem of the navy blue sack dress she wore now was mottled with dried white paste. Was the dinner invitation worth all this trouble? She rubbed the white spots against each other and did the best she could to wipe off the rest with a wet rag. Deciding it passed inspection, she set out with the children.

Dr Kim's home was easy to find without recourse to the meticulous map Kilmo had sketched for her. 'It's right across the street from the mayor's residence,' he had explained. 'It has a huge garden and the second storey is covered in wisteria. You'll have no trouble finding it.' The area was known as the Official Neighbourhood. The homes tended to be opulent and bright sunlight lingered longer there than on other hilltop neighbourhoods. The distinctive design of the home, one of the few of its kind in the city, drew the eye. Two winters ago, with the boy on her back – he had sprained his ankle sledding on ice – she had passed it on her way to the acupuncturist's office. A neighbour had volunteered to escort her – she was terrible with directions – and at the crest of the hill had pointed out the solitary two-storey house sitting far back in the garden.

'You know Dr Kim's Clinic in Chungang-dong, right?' she said in an undertone. 'That's his house.'

Registering the woman's secretive tone, she had observed the brick building with a leery feeling. It resembled a large box with a smaller box stacked on top. It looked sturdy, more like a barracks than a home, and it lacked any indication of vision or affection on the part of the builder – an impression originating perhaps in the tangle of grey wisteria vines camouflaging the facade. The balcony was covered in snow, layered with fallen leaves.

'It's not much to look at in autumn and winter, but it's quite a sight in summer. The fragrance from the wisteria blossoms is nice, but what's really special is the greenery all around it. That's why it's called Green Mansion.'

She had briefly imagined the old, crude, barren, almost

hideous two-storey house that was void of ornamentation turning into a verdure-covered mansion, and had shuddered. 'It must be crawling with bugs!' she said dismissively to her awe-struck, envious neighbour. She had attended middle school and high school in brick buildings dating back seventy or eighty years. Those Western-style buildings with their gables were covered in ivy, and even on the hottest days before summer break the girls were afraid to open the windows lest the caterpillars that swarmed the windowsills crawled inside. From a distance each of those ivy-covered buildings resembled a giant reptile with glinting scales. When the ivy trembled in the breeze she would murmur, 'Oh look, the monster is twitching and shedding.'

Their taxi climbed the gradual slope of the well-paved street that skirted the wall of the primary school and arrived at the crest of the hill.

She recognized the home – the leaves hadn't yet fallen from the vines – but remained at the half-open gate, hesitant to ring the bell. Not knowing either Dr Kim or his wife, hearing the rowdy voices, and seeing the bright lights, she felt a sudden urge to go back.

A young woman appeared at the gate. Had she heard the taxi arriving?

'Well, please come in!' But in the woman's gaze, sweeping over this guest clutching a child with each hand, Myŏnghye read, *Who are these people?*

'Oh, we're with Professor Yi Kilmo . . .' Embarrassed, she couldn't help blushing.

'Ah yes. Thank you for coming. I'm the lady of the house. It's so nice to meet you! And your children . . .'

The woman broke out in a smile and gave the children

a gentle pat on the cheek. In spite of the cool evening she wore a low-cut dress of lightweight fabric. It's so beautiful, thought Myŏnghye as she eyed the fair, smooth skin of the woman's neck, unadorned with a necklace, and recalled that she was the doctor's second wife, was twenty years his junior, and had borne him no children. The garden was larger than it appeared from the street. The light from the lamp posts along the wall and the party lights strung among the shrubbery was warm and inviting. Quite a crowd, thought Myŏnghye; then again, the gathering was well under way. And not exactly the small dinner party she had anticipated.

'You didn't have trouble finding us, I hope?'

'Not at all. I mentioned the mayor's residence and the taxi brought us right here!'

'Like they say, big mountains cast great shade, so thanks be to our illustrious neighbour!' And with that the lady of the house led the new arrivals to the centre of the garden and a large, round table draped with white linen. 'I'd like you to meet the man of the house.' Who proved to be an attractive gentleman with salt-and-pepper hair who was pouring draft beer. With a broad smile he offered Myŏnghye his hand. She allowed her fingers to brush the hand only long enough to feel its warmth and softness. It gave her an impression of generosity and forgiveness.

She heard another vehicle pull up outside. With a brief nod the lady of the house scurried off toward the gate. Myŏnghye heard the familiar greeting: 'Here you are. Please come in. Will your good wife be joining us? You didn't have trouble finding us, I hope?'

Apart from the large, linen-covered table with the food, there were several smaller tables with beer and spirits, cups and glasses, and snacks. Off to one side meat was grilling. The glasses and the stack of white porcelain plates gave off a clean sparkle and in the deepening darkness the lights were all the more splendid. Each of the guests gathered around the tables cast a long shadow on the lawn or along the wall, making those who were circulating appear more numerous than the actual number of guests. Feeling all alone amid the billow of jolly laughter, busy gestures and boisterous greetings, Myŏnghye roved in search of Kilmo. Faces flashed by and she heard a recurring dialogue: *Haven't I seen her before? No, you couldn't have.* The children, anxious and dazed by the unfamiliar setting, clung to her skirt.

And there was Kilmo next to one of the tables, talking with an obese middle-aged man in a raincoat. From the back her husband looked so unsophisticated she could scarcely recognize him. As always happened if she chanced to encounter a family member outside the home, she felt sad, wanted the next instant to avoid the person, and made a face. Some time ago, coming across Kilmo on a busy street, she had quickly looked down and moved out of sight.

Not until Kilmo turned to set an empty glass on a table did he notice her. He produced an awkward *Is that you?* smile, then introduced her to the man in the raincoat.

'Oh my, it's so nice to meet you! I understand you're a writer.'

Kilmo introduced him as Professor Chŏng, explaining that they taught at the same university, whereupon the man grinned from ear to ear, his mouth open as if he were sighing in ecstasy. His grin had the peculiar effect of making him seem to her the nicest man in the world.

Thinking the lights were illuminating her forehead and that Kilmo pitied his wife who was neither young nor pretty, she turned away just enough to prevent the spider web of wrinkles and flawed skin on her unadorned face from being mercilessly exposed.

'Are you hard at work on a story?' said the professor, addressing both of them with the same sugary grin. 'Your good husband must be quite the rock for his wife the writer.'

'Yes, I suppose so,' she could only mumble while wringing her hands together nervously.

The writer tag had been applied a few years back by acquaintances after she received a commendation award in the fiction category of a writing contest sponsored by a daily newspaper. That the awardee was a mother-to-be in her final trimester had added a bit of spice to the short article accompanying the news of the award. The prize money was half what the grand-prize winner would have received, but for her a considerable sum nonetheless. With it she had a new suit made for Kilmo, who had been wearing the same suit all four seasons, bought a pretty crib she had eyed for Yunjae, the baby yet to be born, and provided for herself a huge, sturdy desk from a woodworking shop. These gifts made for a pleasant memory.

People had questioned her with knee-jerk cynicism ever since: *Are you still writing? What're you working on these days?* But the questions had become less frequent. Her response was invariably to smile or mumble ambiguously, allowing her interrogators to interpret after their own fashion, but the questions always left her with clammy palms. She was fearlessly confident that she had a writer's eye for any topic, and yet she was lucky if she published a story a year. And though she considered a small success more worrying than a miserable failure, the stories faded into oblivion with no hint of success or failure. But there were no what-ifs or regrets. Because each publication was one small creative step toward a great leap forward. When she contemplated a story-in-waiting, life felt enriched by the profound implication, apt metaphor and heightened symbolism cached in the kitchen notebook.

Until late each night she sat at her lamp-lit desk sifting through impressions and tracing the tangled chain of her past and future with the present of others, hoping the vitality evoked thereby would come to nuanced life, and she would ultimately commit a few words to paper. But the life that appeared on the blank pages was a succession of trivial days and a stream of convention. Every story was utterly childish and ordinary. But she didn't give up the nightly session at her desk. She suffered terrible eye-strain and was forever exchanging the light in the lamp for a brighter one. But her eyesight remained dim and her eyes, vulnerable to the incandescent bulb, continued to ooze tears.

One night Kilmo had awakened, discovered her hard at work, and, squinting in the lamplight, had said, 'Here you are, engraving again!' That had become his constant comment.

Engraver? This was quite a stretch coming from kill-joy Kilmo. She worried about the liquid oozing from her eyes in the harsh light, fearing he would think she was crying or else fantasize that she was trying to move his heart.

A slender young man with thick eyebrows joined the conversation while tamping down tobacco in the bowl of his pipe: 'That reminds me of something cool one of my profs said: those poor Greeks, they never knew how much fun it is to have a smoke while you're reading a story.' He added he had just completed his internship and been posted at the local District Prosecutor's office. The young prosecutor and the two professors exchanged brief greetings and handshakes.

He then turned to her. 'I've never been big on stories, but it's an honour to meet you!' Tucking his pouch of tobacco in his pocket, he took a delicious pull on his pipe and added, 'Maybe my brain's wired differently, but I find myself reading *nonfiction* rather than fiction.' He smiled the innocent smile of a man who is all too aware of its effectiveness, as if to say, *Forgive me if I'm being too honest.*

She rubbed her forehead for no good reason and recalled some of the random images from her notebook – the white bird, the trilobites fossilized tens of thousands of years ago far below ground level, the blind masseur with the dark glasses she'd encountered in a deserted plaza and the music from his reed flute.

'May you write your heart out, make a name for yourself and earn a bundle of money! Then you can supply the good professor with a nice herbal booster. . . . So please allow me to offer you a drink.' And with yet another smile befitting the world's nicest man, Professor Chŏng filled a glass to the brim with beer and extended it to her.

The children were still clinging to her. She provided each of them with a glass of juice before sipping enough from her own glass to prevent overflow. How happy she had been preparing the cute, cozy cradle and waiting for her baby to be born. And once again she told herself it wasn't so bad to have a drink now and then. The drink she sometimes had during the day when Kilmo was teaching soothed her edgy nerves and offered an escape from the frequent sense of failure, the fretfulness and anxiety she experienced.

The children, pockets bulging with the peanuts and raisins with which the prosecutor had stuffed them, released their grip on their mother's skirt and ran off into the swaying shadows. All the while, cars could be heard arriving and guests could be seen entering. The kitchen ladies in their white aprons scurried nonstop to keep the tables supplied with food.

'Please help yourself to the food and drinks! We have plenty on hand,' announced the lady of the house, who followed up by making a round of the tables. She approached Myŏnghye and drew her close. 'Come, please, there are so many people I'd like you to meet.'

The grill was heaped with burning charcoal. Nearby was yet another small table set with drinks and glasses. A dozen or so women were gathered there, some standing and tending to the meat, others sitting and eating. A porky lady in a black velvet outfit made room for her.

The lady of the house made introductions. 'Mrs Dentist Han, Mrs Professor Im, Madam Nam the craft artist, Madam Chu the painter,' followed by so-and-so's spouse and such-and-such's good wife. Myŏnghye bowed to each in turn. Some looked as youthful as college students, others appeared to be in their fifties.

'As we like to say, three drinks for the new arrival,' proclaimed the woman in black velvet, who turned out to be a six-year member of a ladies' tennis club, and thus nicknamed Lady Game, and the wife of a bank director. Taking a hefty bottle of spirits she winked at the lady of the house. And then to Myŏnghye, 'Here's to you. Mrs Kim has dipped into their private reserve for this special occasion. Or perhaps you'd prefer beer? Then again, this is a close cousin of wine . . .'

'Oh, thank you, but I get kind of wild when I drink . . .' Myŏnghye's response was met with brief titters.

'No worries as long as you don't get physical.'

'Not physical but still ugly,' she confessed. 'I get all weepy.'

'A drink and a few tears are charming, you know.'

'And there are plenty of chivalrous men-of-the-house to look after us, so why not take it to the limit and have all the fun you want?' So saying, the lady of the house poured the orange spirit into champagne glasses and passed them around. The drink had a potent aroma and was hot and bitter to Myŏnghye's parched mouth. To wash away the bitterness she gulped what remained of her beer.

'It's not as easy as I thought to lose weight,' said Lady Game. 'On the tennis court they call me the Flying Pork-Belly.'

'First time I played, they called me the Flying Pig. But Flying Pork-Belly? That's so mean.'

The women cackled, perhaps imagining a portly woman with a tennis racket waddling after a ball.

Myŏnghye was the saviour of their broken conversation. 'What a lovely garden! On a night like this it gives me a really special feeling.'

The lady of the house responded with a bright grin. 'We hoped the wisteria would still be in bloom, but here we are with only the leaves remaining. I can't live with myself unless we do this several times a year. It's a kind of malady, I guess. Anyway, this might be our last *p'at'i* of the year.' And with that she left to refill the ice bucket.

And now Myŏnghye understood: it was a family tradition.

The next thing she knew, Yunjae had returned from his romp around the garden grimacing from a scratch on his face from a rose bush. He burst out crying, and practically the next moment Dr Kim had produced a hand saw and was cutting off the offending bush at its stout base.

'What a waste!' the guests lamented.

The college-lookalike wife of the prosecutor drew close, swirling the liquid in her champagne glass but not deigning to taste it. She obviously found the gathering boring and stupid. A trumpet concerto was blaring from the speaker.

'Well, what do you know – Haydn. I listen to him in the morning, but he sounds a bit different at night. Sounds like a bugle – you know, rise and shine?'

Myŏnghye merely said yes in response. She felt the warmth from the spirit she'd gulped circulating inside her.

'I've only been here three months – tagged along with hubby. I'm kind of worried – I just can't get used to it here, I'm not forming attachments – maybe I was just brought up differently.'

Myŏnghye eyed the pretty lips whenever the woman opened them to speak, thinking she would do well as a toothpaste model. She poured herself another glass of the spirit. The bottle had been left near the grill and the liquid had warmed. The lady of the house hadn't returned with the ice bucket. Sipping her drink ever so slowly, almost licking it, she nodded slowly and deliberately. *Makes sense, I guess.* Flush with the alcohol, she couldn't help but agree.

Charcoal was fed to the dying embers and a cheerful crackle erupted, like that of fireworks. The women jerked back, out of reach of the sparks. The burning coals lent their tipsy faces a gorgeous glow and a vibrant sheen. Myŏnghye pulled her skirt down to conceal the specks of paste that had reappeared there. But she wasn't aware of the paste spots in clear view on her elbows. The boy had crawled up onto a decorative boulder, clinging Tarzan-like to a boxwood shrub nicely pruned by Dr Kim. The girl had followed unsteadily, then fallen, and was crying out for mummy.

'Aha, you have two little ones,' said the craft artist.

'Hmm – well, I'm wondering now if I should have stayed home.' She still hadn't figured out the purpose of the gathering or what the guests had in common; they varied in age and profession and didn't seem especially close with one another.

'I don't think so. What they want to do is convert us from professors to bureaucrats.'

The voice and the topic – independence in academia – were familiar. She looked back and saw Kilmo. His loud voice had brought a temporary hush to the surroundings. The tipsier he was, the louder his voice tended to be. Startled at the volume, his counterpart turned to the others with a subtle *no worries* wave of the hand – a gesture Myŏnghye interpreted as *This guy's clueless* – then returned to Kilmo with an *I'm all ears* expression.

'Everyone is afraid to take issue with what really

matters,' continued Kilmo. 'The heart of the matter is . . .'
The rest was drowned out by the trumpet and the chatter
of the guests. Or had Kilmo lowered his voice in embar-
rassment, realizing he sounded like a boom-box?

'Ma'am,' said Mrs Professor Im to Myŏnghye. 'Did
Professor Song's wife come looking for you too?'

'Professor Song's wife?'

'You know, the sociology professor,' said the woman
in an undertone. 'The one who quit last spring . . .'

'She came by *our* place,' chimed in Lady Game. 'We
went to the same secondary school, you know.'

'No wonder,' said Mrs Dentist Han with a knowing
expression. 'If she's going to visit us just because our kids
go to the same primary school, she's certainly not going
to skip an old classmate.'

'She even saw my husband at his office. Seems she's
calling on every person she knows.'

'Well, she's got to make a living. I feel kind of sorry
for her.'

Hadn't that professor and Kilmo gone to the same
high school? Myŏnghye asked herself. But then a school
connection wasn't so special these days.

'But what's her angle?'

'She sells insurance. So I thought the least I could
do, since I know her, was buy a policy that covers the
kids' education. I'm sure she'll be knocking at your door
before long.'

'A tall tree catches the wind, doesn't it?'

'Isn't that the truth. . . What a bull-headed decision.
Standing on principle won't put food on the table. Why
does his family have to suffer?'

'So what's he been doing with himself?'

'Does the odd translation is what I hear. But the family's having such a terrible time he's even thinking of learning how to drive. Imagine, a man from the ivory tower driving a taxi. It's been less than a year and she's aged a lifetime.'

'I feel for them,' whispered Mrs Professor Im to Myŏnghye with a sigh. 'We'll be in the same fix if hubby ever quits. But you really have to watch your step in academia.'

The women then shifted from old-age couch potato insurance, discussed in hushed tones and sprinkled with such terms as *sacrifice*, *eradication*, and *government policy*, to the new commonhold lifestyle.

The voices buzzing and then fading away and the rippling, affectionate images of the other guests were, for Myŏnghye, red alerts. But she poured herself another drink and had a sip: amid the inevitable tension of this unfamiliar and unsettling atmosphere she would grow no tipsier no matter how much she drank, and none of the women around the grill would notice her consumption.

The meat was tender and perfectly seasoned. The smoke from the grill veiled the sky, and the oak charcoal glowed brightly. She called the children and fed them morsels of meat.

'Meat should be cooked over charcoal . . .'

'No, that's already old school,' said the lady of the house gently. 'We're putting in a barbecue next year. So, let's get together again when the wisteria blooms!'

The children had dutifully drunk whatever their mother gave them and now they were whimpering that they had to pee.

'Why don't you take them out back to the sewer

drain,' said the lady of the house. 'That way you don't have to bother taking off your shoes to go inside.'

Leading to the backyard was a dark, narrow passage between the outer wall and the side of the house. Partway along was a sizable kennel, its opening practically flush with the wall. The trapped dog growled at the human presence; it must have been pacing as well – the chain leash extending from the opening raked nonstop against the cement pathway. Myŏnghye cringed. For all she knew, it must have been trained to behave during parties, but she shuddered nevertheless at the thought of the dog digging its fangs deep into the flesh of her inner thigh. Hoisting the children up, she tiptoed by.

The backyard was just as dark. She heard the rustle of fallen leaves. The garden party was just around the corner behind them, but already the voices and other sounds were distant.

Watching the children relieve themselves of the pent-up liquid, she lifted her skirt and squatted as well. Unlike the front wall with its wisteria façade, the back wall was bare. Here at ground level were the animated sounds of chopping on a cutting board and the whirling of a fan, blending with the murmurs from the party; the first-floor windows were dark and shut except the one at the left corner. Who could that be? Or had someone forgotten to turn off the light? She felt indifferent to the flourishing party out front but was attracted to the lonely light above.

The air was clear and cold. The stars, much more brilliant from here, were telling her that winter loomed. Winter for her meant placing Kilmo's shoes on the warm part of the heated floor before daybreak and breakfast, and taking her asthmatic children, one by the hand and the other piggyback, to the doctor twice a week. And it brought the piercing sorrow she felt gazing at the stars at three in the morning when she went outside to change the coal briquette. In spite of the sweater she'd thrown on, the waning moon and stars, viewed with eyes teary from coughing brought on by the wisps of noxious gas rising from the damp coal briquette, seemed cold and remote. The spiteful, pale blue starlight occasioned a spasm of grief. The frightening stillness that extended from night to dawn was for her a time to count the drops from the leaky tap, a callous silence in which she prayed while striking every match in a box to watch it burst into flame.

Children in tow, she marched back to the party, anxious to suppress any sign of tottering, and to the women next to the grill.

'— so it's true then.' At the sight of Myŏnghye, the craft artist cut short what she was saying. An awkward silence followed.

'It's like a barracks,' said Myŏnghye, indicating the dark upper floor. Revitalized, she nonchalantly poured herself another drink. 'I saw a light on the first floor, but from the outside you can't make out anything else.'

'A light on upstairs – do tell,' said Mrs Prosecutor.

'Yes indeed.'

'Then it's true that their older son is back.'

'Back from . . . overseas?'

'No, not from overseas, from the mental hospital. Hospital, rehab, home – he's always on the move from one place to another.'

Myŏnghye remembered hearing that Dr Kim had three

sons from his first marriage; the oldest had gone abroad while the other two had attended college in Seoul.

'He must be a lot better, then.'

'I heard the Kims don't want outsiders around when he's home. But here they are throwing a party! Makes you wonder – they don't want to excite him, but I guess they're more focused on feeding the rumour mill.'

'Does anyone know the cause?'

'I heard it runs in his family – and that the boy got smacked in the head. But apparently the big issue is family conflict. Anyway, I think I heard he had brain surgery.'

'Someone told me he's anorexic. Won't eat, or if he does, he throws up . . . and they have to put him on an IV.'

'Well, that's easy enough. The lady of the house used to be a shot queen, remember?' This was Mrs Dentist's way of reminding the others that Dr Kim's wife had been a nurse at his clinic not so long ago.

'They think they're keeping it hidden – as they say, it's always darkest beneath the candlestick. But everyone knows.'

'No wonder there's a metal bar across the window,' said Myŏnghye. 'And I think I heard someone groaning.'

'For goodness' sake, is that to keep him from jumping out?' The saucer-eyed women released stifled squeals.

Her fibbing had worked! She toasted herself by gulping the remainder of her drink.

The conjecturing about Dr Kim continued – what they'd seen and heard, what they guessed and imagined – but the voices were much more conspiratorial.

'He's quite the ambitious man, thinking about running for the National Assembly.'

'And why not? He's the right age, he's stashed away a small fortune, and he's well established.'

'Just goes to show you there's no end to a man's desire for power and women.'

And then there were his roles as alumni club president and president of an exclusive private club for promoting regional development and humanitarian service, and his thirty years of investment in local society. All of this combined with the frequent garden parties – and this glitzy one right now was being held out of season and in spite of the son's return home – led them to concur that Dr Kim had in mind the following spring's election. And then there was a sudden, awkward silence that left Myŏnghye wondering if these women had ever met one another before.

The boy was standing precariously on a rock next to the pond, swinging a stick at the water spurting from the fountain as if to cut it in half. *I'd better stop him before he falls in*, she thought. Opening her hazy eyes, she set off toward the pond, walking like a wooden soldier.

'Ma'am. Over here, ma'am!' The voice came from one of the round tables. 'I'd like to offer you a drink. Can't trust a writer who can't drink! Unless you get drunk, how can you write a story about a drunkard?'

It was Professor Chŏng and he looked quite tipsy. *Well, why not? It's not like I turn red in the face after a couple of drinks.* She felt Kilmo's piercing gaze and had to remind herself she'd never been caught drinking during the day. She confidently extended a hand to accept a foaming glass of beer.

'Well, after all, isn't fiction a magnificent lie?' said Chŏng.

'In that case, our honourable writer must be a great liar.'

The group burst into laughter at this great comeback.

'I doubt that – I'm still a rookie!' said Myŏnghye.

Two men opposite her were deep into a discussion of a recent study of carrots and cancer. Hearing the laughter, they looked up, but when the laughter abruptly ended they produced so-what looks and munched on carrots from a just-delivered tray.

'Everyone's scared of cancer but that doesn't mean we have to stop eating.'

The boy was still smacking the water from his precarious perch, sending it flying in all directions. The guests nearby scowled and moved away.

It's just a teeny puddle. He might fall but he won't drown. And then, swelling with Dutch courage, she spoke up: 'I'd like to depict a typical figure of the times: a man who in his prudence is like an inchworm, who in his powers of judgement is like an arthropod that would give up a leg to an enemy in order to escape, who in his power to heal is like a starfish. Needless to say, the story will be heavy on satire—'

'Look this way! And closer together, please!'

She saw Dr Kim thrusting a camera in her direction. 'Perfect!' There was a flash. She felt an arm around her shoulder and by reflex looked up to see Kilmo.

'Here you go, it's a Polaroid. The two of you look so cozy.' And with a chuckle Dr Kim left in search of the next couple.

In the drying photo she was eying Kilmo with a happy smile, glass of beer held high, and Kilmo was wearing a jolly smile. The white smudge of paste on her elbow was faintly visible, but she didn't care.

'Of course,' she continued, 'he gets to enjoy worldly success and power—'

Again she was interrupted by Chŏng. 'Postwar stories are full of characters like that. The times change but the people living through those times have a huge common denominator, yes? That's something else I picked up as an undergrad.'

The prosecutor made a serious face and nodded.

She felt like a shoemaker who always made her shoes the same size. The kids would keep growing and the shoes would never fit – they were useless. She picked up a glass of flat beer left unattended on the table. So what about the white bird flying off into the long, long flow of time between five and six in the afternoon? What about the man on the tightrope slowly going insane from loneliness? Was it any use trying to draw meaningful metaphors of life from them?

Talk of cancer, tennis and jogging, last night's hangover, nuclear war and Nostradamus brushed past Myŏnghye. Someone complained about the pathetic pay you could expect in his profession; someone else said, 'Nice to meet you, hope we can see each other more often'; and someone else expressed contempt about someone not present.

She held her glass at eye level and drank the lukewarm beer. Through the glass she could see little Myŏnghŭi waddling towards the grill looking for Mummy.

And then she brought the glass against her forehead and thought about the time she had spent, the corners she had turned in her quest for any tiny clue that would help actualize the agonizing desire boiling inside her. She had once spent half a day in a slaughterhouse yard watching sunlight pour onto the tin roof as the cattle were led inside. The butcher, descendant of a *paekchŏng*, an outcaste, seemed dispirited. And she had rented a boat and spent a day on an island in a river visiting a prehistoric archaeological site and wondering whether all the pebbles beneath her feet were from that ancient period . . .

From near the grill came the shriek of a child. *Myŏnghŭi.* She set down her glass and approached the girl slowly and, she wished, soberly, hoping her ever so nonchalant and lofty guise might be seen by her hosts as a gesture of etiquette.

'She burned herself on the grill, didn't realize it was hot. I guess nobody noticed how close she was,' said the lady of the house. And with an apologetic and embarrassed expression she transferred the girl to Myŏnghye.

Of course, she thought. The girl was shorter than the grill and must have been hidden from view.

The inside of one of the girl's fingers was red and swollen. Seeing Mummy, she began shrieking.

'Could you bring me some Vaseline?' asked Myŏnghye.

'Alcohol might be better,' suggested Mrs Dentist.

Mrs Prosecutor brought a glass of beer. Myŏnghye rolled up the girl's sleeve and dunked her hand into it.

Kilmo approached, wearing a concerned scowl. 'Myŏnghŭi, are you all right?'

'It's nothing serious,' said Myŏnghye. 'It got singed is all.'

The girl had stopped crying. Sitting meekly on a rock in the garden, hand still in the beer, she looked like a doll. The boy left the fountain to join his sister and with a glum expression began yawning nonstop. It was well past their bedtime.

Two of the kitchen ladies appeared with a small table draped in white cloth. The lady of the house removed the cloth and there was a swell of admiration from the guests. Resting on a pile of large white plates was a gigantic crab.

'Our special treat,' said the lady of the house to the awed assemblage. 'Please help yourselves; otherwise you can't say you've been a guest of ours.'

The kitchen ladies set the plates on the tables and Dr Kim made a circuit of the guests, refilling empty glasses. The cooked crab was bright red but otherwise looked lifelike, its dubious compound eyes looking askance at the asparagus that adorned it all around. The legs were removed, and in no time all that remained was the body with its questioning eyes. The lady of the house expertly removed the back of the shell to reveal the innards along with a dazzling display of white meat.

The smaller and more wretched the body of the crab, the higher the heaps of shells on the tables. And then someone launched into a celebratory song and Dr Kim turned off the stereo.

'We should go. It's past their bedtime,' she said.

Kilmo checked his watch. 'It's not even ten.'

'Oh? Then you can stay and I'll sneak out – but be sure to thank them for me.' And with the girl on her back and the boy by the hand, she slipped behind the other guests.

Kilmo followed them out the gate, hands in his pockets, a sulky look on his face. 'I'll flag down a taxi.' His alcohol-quickened breath reeked of meat smoke and beer. The chorus of the song was audible: 'Listen to the watermill, Maggie – Maggie, my love . . .' Kilmo glanced back at the gate. Seeing a taxi coming up the slope, Myŏnghye nudged him toward the gate. 'The taxi's here, so back you go.'

The taxi came to a stop. *Damn!* She had stuck her wallet

in Kilmo's pocket because her dress had no pockets. She could have followed Kilmo back inside to fetch it but decided instead to walk down the hill, hoping the chilly air would wake her up. Warmed though she was from the drinks, she could feel the temperature dropping. The drastic difference in day- and nighttime temperatures was characteristic of this inland city. Why not add a song of her own to this chilly, soulless street? That way she could clear her head and leave herself much refreshed.

Ahead of her walked a long shadow and a short one. The girl's hands clutching her made the shoulders in the long shadow resemble two small horns. Now and then a taxi ran over the lonesome shadows. Whenever a vehicle passed by, she would totter to the side of the road and the girl would startle awake with a feeble moan.

The wall of the primary school seemed endless. The ground felt like it was moving, causing her to move even more uncertainly; time and again she had to stop and blink. She could still hear singing and still see the bright light from the garden.

'Why isn't Dad with us?' the boy asked sullenly, head hunched over.

Good question – was it the singing? she wondered. 'He's coming. He just wants to talk some more with his friends.'

Kilmo would return late and his hair would be grey. Whenever he came home drunk, his hair looked grey in the streetlight of their alley. After all this time, the sight still frightened her. 'Ah ah, the dreams are gone, the dreams are gone.' Merrily, merrily went their songs about lost youth and vanished dreams and new friend-ships forged by drink. The singing and merriment would continue through the night. How heartwarming the distant songfest; how seductive the distant lights. She had just left and now she wanted to go back to that site full of pleasure and abandon, a place that would stubbornly refuse her entry. She knew that before long and all at once the lights would be extinguished; the women adorned in their lovely lightweight garments would shiver in the sudden chill of night, feel an inexplicable sense of betrayal and shame at the sweet white flesh of the crab and the pile of vivid red shells they had spat out, and then hasten to shake hands and exchange goodbyes; the exhausted lady of the house would rush the kitchen ladies in a tone of irritation; and by the time anyone realized the rose bush was nothing more than an ugly stump, the low growl of the dog and the retching of the crazy young man, which would only upset his already emptied stomach, would fill the garden. Knowing all this, she still wanted to return.

She began talking out loud to herself. 'When I sneaked out without saying goodbye to the lady of the house she must have thought I'd taken the kids out back to pee again. How stupid I am to even think of walking home when the kids are sleepy! It's so chilly and now the wind's picked up!'

The boy kept stealing nervous glances at her.

She turned to go back but had to sag against the school wall to keep from falling. The homes across the street, the tree branches extending over their walls, and the moon suddenly concealed by clouds all turned upside down in a massive handstand. With her free hand she propped up the girl on her back then plopped to the ground. The meat, alcohol and crab she'd stuffed herself with, undigested and rioting, rose to her oesophagus.

Gaping and panting, she regarded the house she had just left. In her rolling field of vision, the house on the hill stood tall like a huge reptile, a cold-blooded Mesozoic creature sprung from its earthen crypt that was thousands of years in the making. It seemed to inch along, scales quivering in the gradually building wind. She had to get the kids home. She tried her best to rise, but the crushing weight of the girl on her back and the ever-present dizziness left her powerless to steady her legs. She resented Kilmo for allowing his drunken wife to leave all by herself with the children, she resented the fact that she was incapable of giving up her dreams, and she resented the meaningless, tear-drenched comfort and feeling of security generated by her tipsiness.

'All right, I had too much to drink. I shouldn't have done that. But I couldn't help it. You probably didn't notice, but all those people were telling me, come on, have a drink. You know, sometimes I get really lonely. Where are we, anyway? Do you remember the way home?'

She rose just enough to take the girl from her back and embrace her, then sank back down. She tugged gently at the boy's ear and managed to draw his tense, rigid body toward her. His large, terror-filled eyes came close.

'Don't worry, we'll be home soon. What a disgusting party – those people are worthless. Let's take a short break. When I was a little girl I used to think the grownups knew *everything*. But look at me, I'm a grownup and sometimes I can't find my way home at night. Strange, isn't it.'

She gave the boy a loving smile to ease his fears. But her eyes were on the hilltop house swaying ever more grandly and looming closer in the darkness beyond his

95

small shoulders. The terror was unbearable and she closed her eyes. Closed them as tightly as she could, not so much from fear of the approaching beast with the quivering scales, but to escape the gaze of the little boy she had terrified with her drunken rambling.